KILLING DR. WATSON

BY MATT FERRAZ

Contents

To my parents

"My heroes had the heart to lose their lives out on a limb
And all I remember is thinking, 'I want to be like them'"

Gnarls Barkley, Crazy

Sherlock Holmes shouted from inside of me: "Show your talent, boy!"

Medeiros e Albuquerque: Se eu fosse Sherlock Holmes

PROLOGUE

The BBC called me again, for the third time this month. The first two times they were at least professional enough to contact me at my office during daytime. This time they called me at home while I was having dinner with my family. I tried to be polite, at least as polite as man can be when the past he's trying to leave behind keeps coming back like this. "No," I said to the TV producer on the other end of the line. "I have no interest in giving you an interview, and would appreciate if you didn't call me again."

"Just listen, Mr. Bellamy," he said, trying to prevent me from hanging up on him. "I realise you feel uncomfortable talking about the case..."

"I wouldn't call it a case," I said. "It was all very childish and very stupid. I was just a kid back then — a kid who watched too much TV."

I didn't mean that as an insult, but wouldn't mind if he took it that way. I haven't watched TV for a long time now. I have too much work to do, too many books to read and two kids who need my attention. I have a TV in the living room and another one in the bedroom, but rarely use them.

"There are a lot of people who want to see this documentary," he said, patiently. "And we are gathering all the information we can on..."

"You have told me all that already," I said. "And I'll give you the exact same answer: I'm not interested in appearing on TV."

"You don't have to make an appearance," the producer said. "We can blur your face or use a body double. We won't identify you."

I sighed. My meal was getting cold, my wife was getting upset and I had no business talking to that man. The best thing would be to hang up on him and stop answering his calls. That's what I should have done from the start. My past was behind me and that's where I'd like it to stay. Each time I thought about it, I realised how dangerous and stupid the whole thing was. It wasn't something I'd be pleased to talk about in front of a camera.

But I kept listening just a bit longer. Because there was a part of me that couldn't forget that case. A part that wanted to tell that story.

"I'm not supposed to tell you this," said the producer after half a minute of silence. "But we can't do this without you. You are the most important source we got about what happened to…"

"Please don't call me again," I said and hung up before he could say any names. I went back to the dining table, leaving the phone off the hook.

"Who was it, Jerry?" my wife asked in a concerned voice.

"It was Kevin again," I said. Kevin Maguire was a colleague of mine who liked to consult me about technicalities. "Jean, stop playing with your food!" I said to my little daughter, just to change subjects.

All that happened a few hours ago, and now I'm having trouble to sleep. Every time I close my eyes I see her face lying on that kitchen floor, with her purple face and black eye. After all those years, she's still on my mind. My wife didn't bother to ask me if there was anything wrong. She stopped doing that after the first year of marriage. I have seen some awful stuff in my life — what grown man hasn't? But none of it has left such an impression on me as my first contact with the real world. That case that almost got me killed.

Now that everyone's sleeping in the house, I've sat in my office with this voice recorder and a pot of strong coffee and will try to purge this whole thing from my mind. That BBC guy would do anything to have this recording, but I don't plan to show this to anyone and will probably erase it after it's finished. Maybe this way I'll erase everything and be able to go on with my life without thinking about everything that happened when somebody started killing Dr Watson.

PART ONE — BROKEN CHINA

CHAPTER ONE

The Fanboy

I was 25 years old the first time I saw Sir Bartholomew Neville in person, at a TV convention in Chelsea in early 1998. It was one of the greatest moments of my life, even though it consisted basically of sitting on a tight chair in a crowded auditorium the whole night while other fans screamed and cheered. I almost didn't make it there in time and was probably the last person to enter the theatre before the doors were closed. I had to skip work, which would probably get me fired the following day. I also had to borrow my brother's car, and was supposed to fill the tank and take it for a wash before returning it. But it's silly to complain when you're about to meet your greatest hero, the man you looked up to throughout your whole adolescence. Granted, in many aspects my adolescence was barely over, but the BBC was still making money with reruns of *The Baker Street Sleuth*. It was beyond my comprehension why they had cancelled the show in the first place. Some magazines said it was because of Bartholomew Neville's harsh temper, but to me that was just gossip. Even if he did have such temper, who cared? He was the best and always would be. To me, getting home from school every afternoon meant sitting in the couch and watching the adventures of Sherlock Holmes and Watson — and no actor had ever played the world's greatest detective as amazingly as Neville.

The Baker Street Sleuth ran for four series, and for each one of those a BAFTA decorated Bartholomew Neville's shelf. The writers seemed to lose most of their creativity by the last series, which was a bit weaker as a result. The mysteries were kind of predictable and the catchphrases were overused, but Neville's performance was as impeccable as ever. And aside from that disappointing final year, there were still those three masterful first series, and they never got old, no matter how many times I watched them.

I was supposed to meet some friends there, if you could call them that. Friends are usually people you share secrets and interests with. *The Baker Street Sleuth* was the only one interest I shared with those guys, and we rarely talked about anything else. Not that it mattered, anyway. Socialization was never my top priority, especially not that night. I had attended many conventions before, but that was the first time I'd be able to share the same room with Sherlock Holmes himself.

The plan was to be the first one in line to enter the auditorium, but the traffic was so heavy it took me forever to arrive there, and the line was already huge. I looked through the line, trying to find someone I knew, when my eyes caught Caesar Ace, one of my least favourite people in the world. In theory we ought to have been best friends, since we were both huge fans of *The Baker Street Sleuth*. But I guess that was what made us so bitter with each other. We were always arguing to see who knew more about the show.

"Hi, Caesar," I said, trying to earn some solidarity. "You must have arrived early."

"Look, if it ain't Jerry Bellamy!" he said. "I thought you worked on nightshift."

"I do," I said, trying to smile. I was a bagger at a quick market; not the most glamorous job in the world, but it paid the bills. Well, some of them. "Listen, I was caught in the traffic. Do you think maybe we…?"

"I didn't know you had a car," Caesar said.

"It's my brother's car," I answered. "Listen, do you think we could…"

"Why don't you try to talk to Andrea?" he said, pointing behind with his thumb. "I know she'll be delighted to see you."

Andrea Linskey was another of our so-called 'friends'. She had short green hair, thick eyebrows and bad breath. Caesar knew I had tried to hit on her at another convention, a couple of months before, and all she did was laugh in my face. I decided not to ask any favours from anyone else and walked to the end of the line, just before the gate was opened. When I got inside, there were no seats left, but I didn't feel like complaining. I was in, and that was what mattered.

The auditorium wasn't very big, but I managed to be fairly close to the stage by sitting in the aisle. I wasn't the only one in that situation, as there were also people standing at the corners, squeezed into the small space between the chairs and the walls.

I was so nervous, sitting on the cold floor in that auditorium, trying to imagine what to say to Neville if, by chance, he noticed my existence. Should I say I was his number one fan? Neville was famous all around the world and had millions of admirers. I loved his stuff, but didn't have the money to buy every product a number one fan was 'supposed' to own. But what wouldn't I do to be able to talk to him face to face, just the two of us! I wouldn't even ask him to sign anything for me; all I wanted was to let him know that, for me, he would always be the best.

"Would you excuse me?"

I looked up and saw a redheaded girl in tweed. She had a serious look in her face and was so beautiful it hurt my eyes. She didn't seem to belong here with the rest of us and didn't strike me as a fan. But then again, it was easy to see that not everyone attending that meeting had seen the show. Most of them, I thought, would be glad just to be in a room alongside a famous person.

I got up to let the redhead pass, and she went quietly to a brunette sitting three chairs from the aisle, about ten feet from where I sat. The redhead girl opened her purse and gave a piece of paper to the brunette.

The brunette read the letter with a face of surprise and delight. She asked the redhead something, but the auditorium was so noisy that she repeated the question in a louder voice. "The usual?" Her voice was sharp and sounded like fingernails against a blackboard.

The redhead nodded and said: "You can go. I'll take your place."

The brunette collected her stuff and walked out. As she passed me on her way to the exit, her purse hit me in the face. The brunette didn't seem to care and just kept walking. I yelled something at her, but she was already gone. I turned back my head and saw that she had left a piece of paper on the floor. I picked it up and put it in my pocket without looking at it.

The redheaded girl sat in her place and, as though that was his cue, the host appeared onstage and I lost interest in her. My idol was about to appear in front of me, after a forty-minute delay; by the time he finally came on I was hungry, sleepy and needed to go to the toilet, but I wouldn't have left my spot for the world. Other fans were starting to get angry, but I wasn't. If the greatest actor in the world was willing to grace us with his presence, however briefly, it was our duty to stay put. And if he needed a few more minutes, who were we to complain?

When the host said: "Ladies and gentlemen, Sir Bartholomew Neville", the crowd fell silent. The lights changed. We saw his shadow first, stretching out from the back of the stage. Then somebody spotted the tip of his pipe. The man was there, in his deerstalker hat and plaid cape, the pipe in his left hand, the magnifying glass in his right. His nose was as thin as it was on TV, his face even bonier. And his walk — what a walk! Like a cat that pretends nonchalance when he knows he's the centre of attention and is enjoying every minute of it. The announcer was wrong; it wasn't Bartholomew Neville up there, it was Sherlock Holmes in the flesh.

Suddenly, we were all cheering. People clapped, whistled, yelled, but the man just stood there, pretending to smoke his unlit pipe, as though he didn't see us. There wasn't any space in his brilliant mind for all that noise. People had their cameras in their hands, taking pictures, but they were missing the real thing. He remained there and waited until we were finished. Then he sat in a chair by the host's side.

"Good evening, Sir Bartholomew."

"Thanks, Josh," he said. "It's a pleasure to be here."

You'd think that calling Neville by his real name would make him break character, but it didn't. Neither did the questions about his career and personal life. It was like seeing Holmes answering questions for a completely different person. When the host, Josh, asked Neville about an episode in the second series, he answered as the detective responsible for solving that particular crime, not as the actor who had played a role and followed a script. We were all mesmerised.

The first questions were about Neville's latest works. He had played Iago in a small production of *Othello*, but it had only lasted for one season. He'd also been in talks to play Van Helsing in a new Dracula movie and had been considered for a starring role in a new series about the adventures of an archaeologist. None of these projects had thrived, but then, Neville wasn't here to talk about these roles. The audience, including myself, soon started to get impatient; the host, sensing this, finally turned his attention to what really mattered.

"What was your favourite episode of *The Baker Street Sleuth*?"

"My favourite case is always the one I'm in currently", answered Sir Bartholomew. "But since you have to ask, I took a great deal of pleasure investigating the Henry Baskerville case."

"That's the Hound of the Baskervilles, everyone!" said the host. Like we didn't know that already. Goddamn it, was Josh the host really the best person they could find for the job of interviewing Bartholomew Neville? "How did you feel about being off-screen for most of the episode?"

"I took a different approach on that case," said Neville. "Some people believe I should have been more direct, but my absence was crucial to preventing Sir Henry from falling victim to that dreadful conspiracy."

"Isn't it true that you have demanded more screen time from your agent?"

For an extremely brief second I saw Neville's look. I don't know if anyone else saw it, but in that moment, an expression of hatred flickered across his face. It was so fast that I thought maybe I'd imagine it, and it would be a long time before I remembered it again.

The glimpse of Neville was fleeting; soon it was Sherlock Holmes again on the stage. He put his pipe aside and gave a great answer. "Time is crucial in a case like that," he said, referring again to the Baskerville case. "If I could somehow find more time, I most certainly would."

The crowd applauded and the host tried not to look too stupid. He finally realised how clueless he was about the whole subject and let Neville guide the rest of the interview, asking vague questions and letting the great man work his magic. After some time, he turned questions over to the audience. We all raised our arms; some raised both. Neville studied every raised hand before pointing to a bald guy in the last row; he was wearing a Pierce Brosnan James Bond t-shirt, a golden watch and giant glasses.

"You, sir," Neville said. "Let's hear what you have to say." He paused and added, "I sincerely doubt you've ever seen an episode of *The Baker Street Sleuth*; I think it rather more likely that your presence here may be explained by a desire to obtain an autograph for your daughter's birthday."

With that, we were silent again. Neville slowly filled his pipe with fresh tobacco.

"How do you know that?" the bald man asked, after a moment of dumbfounded silence.

Neville smiled as he tamped down the tobacco. "That t-shirt you're wearing," he said. "It's three sizes too big and has never been worn before. You bought it ten minutes ago, at reception, and not because you're a fan of James Bond. There were plenty of Bond t-shirts in many sizes, but you selected a *Tomorrow Never Dies* print that doesn't fit — probably because the film is being released this month, and it's all over the media. Even a non-Bond fan such as yourself must be familiar with that movie." He clamped the pipe between his teeth and spoke around it. "You were trying to fit into the crowd, but you clearly stand out. You are here exclusively to get an autograph. I can see you have a briefcase with you and that you've already taken a shower. That must mean you've already checked out of the hotel and are going directly to the airport after this event. You were in London for business, but decided to come by and get this autograph for your daughter. I believe it's her birthday tomorrow, since you couldn't afford to spend another night in London, even to get a better night's sleep."

"And how did you know I have a daughter instead of a son?" he asked.

"Am I right?" Neville asked.

"Well, yes," said the man.

"Do come here," said Neville. "Let me sign this for you."

Everybody cheered. The man didn't even get to ask his question. He got his autograph and practically ran away from the auditorium, clearly spooked by Neville's eerie insight. We all were, to some extent; it was uncanny how much Sir Bartholomew seemed to parallel his fictional counterpart. Far fewer hands were raised as the host asked for another question. One of those hands was mine, of course, but again I wasn't selected. They pointed to someone in the row next to me, and I wasn't pleased to see Caesar Ace getting up.

"Sir Bartholomew," he said. "There has been a debate amongst fans regarding how many different actors played Watson in the show. Most people believe there are only three, and the official guides agree on that, but in the original airing of *The Final Problem*..."

"I'm sorry," said Josh. "But I was pointing to the girl next to you."

Lots of people laughed, and I was one of them. It was great to see Ace so embarrassed, especially when he was trying to show off. Josh had selected the girl sitting right next to Ace: the redhead I'd seen earlier. She got up and for a moment the whole auditorium fell silent. When she spoke, there was some fear in her voice.

"I know this is weird, Sir Bartholomew," she said, voice shaking. "But I'm here because I need you to find the man who killed my father."

The girl twisted a handkerchief in her small fingers.

"I'm sorry," said the host quickly, looking alarmed at her words and clearly eager to cut her off before she said anything else. "I think we'd better end things here."

Neville stared at her for a long time, and then, with trembling hands, he lit his pipe. Little by little, Sherlock Holmes drained out of his face. It was like he had met her before. When he spoke, his voice was completely different.

"Do I know you?" he asked.

"My name is Lucy Ferguson," she said, looking up at him. "And I…"

"Please," said the host, trying and failing to control the situation. The auditorium was buzzing with people whispering back and forth, but Ms Ferguson just stood there, looking directly up into Neville's eyes. The host, making one final attempt to gain control, said, "I think we must…"

He was interrupted by the loud shriek of the fire alarm. Ms Ferguson tried to speak again, but the host had already grabbed Neville by the arm and was propelling him towards the door. I caught three words out of Lucy Ferguson's mouth: "at the second". As the crowd surged towards the exits, I ran to Ms Ferguson. It wasn't the wisest thing to do, but my instincts told me that she was in danger. She stood still, seemingly oblivious to the alarm, and if there were a real fire she probably would burn to death. My own actions were courageous but stupid: as I ran towards her, a little voice in my head reminded me that I could die trying to save someone I didn't know. But something in that whole situation smelled, and it wasn't because of smoke.

I was moving against the crowd and had to force my way through, elbowing any number of people as I went. We weren't that far apart from each other, but the crowd was too large, and I was running against it. I briefly lost sight of her as I put my head down and pushed forward; when I came back up and refocused my attention on the space she'd occupied, Lucy Ferguson was no longer there.

We all gathered in the street and stared at the building, trying to see some fire, but there was no sign of it. It didn't take much time for everyone to realise it had been a false alarm. We all wanted to go back inside and continue the event, but they wouldn't let us. I tried to find Lucy Ferguson amongst the crowd, but she had disappeared.

CHAPTER TWO

Jackson's Dove

The next day's papers mentioned the fake fire alarm, but there was nothing about Mrs Ferguson. The leading theory was that some prankster had pushed the alarm button in the hallway leading to the lobby in an attempt to spread panic. There wasn't any solid evidence, but a woman who had requested anonymity claimed that when she was on her way to the bathroom she'd seen a tall man standing in the lobby, just two minutes before the alarm went off.

I didn't get any sleep that night; Lucy Ferguson constantly haunted my thoughts. It wasn't just that she was one of the most beautiful women I'd ever seen. No, there was something else. Something very odd. First, there was the way she'd taken the place of the brunette. Did that mean something? Then there was the way the host had acted when Lucy had appealed to Neville. It hadn't been just surprise; he'd been angry, like he had been betrayed. What did that mean? And then, of course, there was the request itself. I couldn't speak from experience, but it seemed to me a given that if your father's murdered, you don't demand assistance from an actor, or in front of so many people; the police, or a private investigator, surely can give a lot more help. Maybe Lucy Ferguson's admiration for Neville as Holmes had ventured into delusions, and she wasn't able to tell that Neville and Holmes were not one and the same?

'The usual' — that was what the brunette had said, and even now her voice pounded in my ears. Whatever the usual was, it was enough to take her out of her seat. I tried to force my memory, extract any detail from what I'd seen. Had the letter been in some kind of envelope, or had Ms Ferguson taken it out of her pocket?

What colour was the paper? I did remember one thing: the way the brunette had said those two words. She'd been asking, hadn't she? She'd been asking, but not in the way you'd expect. It had been as if she were surprised by the usual. As though the usual meant something important to her.

I woke up late, still dressed in the same clothes, and decided to drive around and think. My shift wouldn't start until later that day, but after last night, I wanted to arrive a little early. My brother would need the car before lunch, but I still had a few more minutes to fill the tank. On my way to the petrol station, I turned on the radio; they were repeating everything that had already been said about the previous night's events. I was barely paying attention until a kind of familiar voice started talking.

"My name is Angela, Angela Dove."

"Where are you calling from, Angela?" asked the anchor-man.

"I'm in Soho, but last night I was at that theatre, and I know who pushed that alarm button. I don't know her name, but the bitch took me out of my place…"

"Ms Dove, please remember that we are live on air."

"I don't give a shit! I was there doing a gig, and she made me go away just so she could take my place, that little…"

They cut her off at that point and start talking about soccer. Angela Dove. I had recognised the voice. Now I had a name for the brunette. I went to the next phone booth and looked for her name in the book. It was a dead end: there was no Angela Dove in Soho. I sighed and closed the phone book, but then remembered of something: the piece of paper she let fall on the floor the previous night. It was still in my pocket. It was a restaurant card and had a number on it. I went back to the phone booth and dialled the number

"Juliano's Brazilian Food," said a deep male voice. "This is Lucas. How can I help you?"

For a moment I was so surprised I almost hung up, but then I asked if I could speak to Angela Dove.

"Who wants to speak with her?" he asked.

I gave it some thought. My first instinct was to say I was from Scotland Yard, but if he didn't believe me, he'd hang up on my face. "I'm her brother," I said.

"Is this urgent, sir?" he asked. "She can't take personal calls right now."

"Why not?" I asked. "Is it because she was calling a radio station a few moments ago?"

"I can't give you that information," he said. "And if you're not going to order something, I…"

I hung up and went back to my car. Everything was out of place. I had one woman taking the place of another. A letter. A weird request. A fire alarm. A gig. Nothing unusual about any of those. Then why was I so intrigued by the whole thing?

There was still a little time, I drove to Soho and decided to have some Brazilian for lunch. Juliano's Brazilian was very busy, but I found a place in a corner and ordered some rice and beans. The place was a mess, like the cleaning lady wasn't doing her best efforts to keep the place clean.

A door in the corner swung open and a woman came out; I recognised her as the brunette from the previous night, though now she seemed a lot less glamorous. Her angry face made her look a bit older. I left my untouched lunch on the table and went to her.

"What do you want?" she asked. "Make it quick. I'm having a lousy week."

"My name is Jerry Bellamy, Ms Dove, and I want to have a word with you," I said. She looked at me with tired eyes, and there was some hope in them.

"You came over here just to talk with me?" she asked.

"Well, there are some very important matters I want to discuss…"

"Have we met before?" she asked.

"I saw you in a theatre…"

She took me by the hand and took me into the street. "We can't have a proper conversation here," she said, leading the way. "There's a nice café around the corner where we can talk."

I tried to say something as we went, but she just wouldn't shut up. "I couldn't stand working in that place anymore," she said. "The manager got furious just because I made a quick call. Thankfully you arrived! I believe this is a sign from heaven!"

I was confused and tried to talk to her, but she just wouldn't listen. Thankfully the café was nearby. Angela made me sit down and ordered something.

"I have been in three plays, including a production of *Caligula*," she said.

"Please, I don't…"

"I also was on this fringe festival here," she said, interrupting me as she found a folder in her purse and handed it to me. It had pictures of a tiny stage and a tiny figure that I assumed must be her. "I've done many auditions for movies and TV, but theatre is really my thing." She looked excited. "I can do Lady Macbeth if you want."

"I'm sorry," I said, "I think you've confused me with someone else."

Her smile faded.

"You're not a theatre agent?"

I stared at her. "A what?"

"Damn!" she cried, loudly. I could almost feel my ears bleeding. "And I thought my week was starting to get good."

"Why'd you think I was a theatre agent?"

"You said you saw me in a theatre and called me Angela Dove," she said, taking the folder from my hand and returning it to her purse. "It's my stage name." She looked annoyed and added, "If you'll excuse me, I have to find a new job."

She started to get up, but I grabbed her by the hand and made her sit down again.

"Hang on. I wanted to talk to you."

"Okay," she said "What do you want?"

The barman came by with two cups of coffee and served us. I waited for him to be gone, like we were discussing some top secret stuff. "I know about the usual," I finally said.

Her mouth formed a perfect O. Then she covered her face with her hands and sighed. Her hands dropped and she picked up her coffee before looking at me again. All of this in about only five seconds.

"That was so embarrassing," she said. "I'd report that carrot top to the police if I knew her name. You know how much they were paying me? Thirty quid! Thirty quid just to raise my hand and ask some stupid question. 'Sir Bartholomew, do you smoke pipes in real life?'"

I was starting to understand where that was going. Too bad I didn't pay much attention to the content of that question at the moment. Things might have turned different if I did. "You mean the questions were...?" I was unable to finish the question.

"Staged? Of course, didn't you know that?"

"No, I didn't," I said slowly. "I thought..."

"Oh, you poor thing!" she said. "You thought that piece of ham on the stage really had all those deductive powers?" She looked at me pityingly. "How else do you think they could amaze everyone in the audience?"

It made sense, though I'd never thought Sir Bartholomew would do something like that. It totally broke the enchantment of having met him.

"It was safe cash," she continued, "but they won't pay me. The carrot top said she was my replacement, and that I had gotten a role in *Who's Afraid of Virginia Woolf*, at the Usual Company. She said they needed me at their offices as soon as possible to sign the contract. I got there, and they didn't even know who I was!" She looked furious. "And the carrot top is now thirty quid richer. I wonder if that's her thing: going around and stealing other people's gigs."

I was still trying to piece everything together. "Why did you believe her?"

"She gave me this letter."

Angela pulled a piece of paper from her purse and handed it to me — the same piece of paper that Lucy Ferguson had handed her the previous night, I supposed. It had the signature and the stamp of Mr Terence Holdwood: Director of the Usual Company.

"Can I keep this?" I asked.

"What for?"

"It's important," I said, dodging the question.

"Help yourself," she said. "And if you do find her, please give her this message."

Angela slapped me in the face and went away.

CHAPTER THREE

A Very Unusual Company

I called the Usual Company as soon as Angela was gone and the manager said I could swing by at six o'clock. Since my shift started at six, I called my boss to say I'd be an hour late.

He was not happy to hear this. "Do you think I can't find anyone who'd pack groceries better than you, Bellamy?" he said with his raspy voice. "Do you think you have some kind of special talents that mean the business will fall apart without you?"

"I'm sorry, Mr Goodwill," I said. Yes, that was really his name. "But this is a matter of…"

"Yesterday it was a matter of going to some nerdy convention and taking pictures with Roger Moore," he said, cutting me off.

"Actually…"

"Don't actually me," he said sharply. "But I'll tell you what. I'll give you another chance. I need someone to keep an eye on the store during the holidays. Seems like a job for you. Assuming you'll still be working for me until then."

"I guess I probably will." I didn't really have anything else to say.

"And," he continued, "this is the last time I'm going to be this fucking nice. One more and you're out."

"That won't happen, sir."

"Okay," he said, sounding much more cheerful. "Have a nice day, you goddamn weirdo."

I got in my car, thinking my day could be worse...and then realised that it wasn't my car. For the thousandth time that day, I went back to the phone booth.

My brother was furious. "I told you I needed the car today, Jerry!"

"I know, Pete," I said. "I just have a lot to do."

That wasn't an easy thing for me to say. Pete was the responsible brother, the one who had a real job and a family. When he said he needed the car, he wasn't talking about pursuing some hot redhead like me; he was talking about picking his kids up at school and going to the store to buy diapers.

"Can you at least tell me what it is?" he asked.

"Not right now," I said. I could feel his frustration through the phone. "It may be nothing. Please, Pete, I'll do anything you ask. I'll buy you new tires if you want. Just let me have it tonight."

He was silent for a moment before finally saying, "What I really want, Jerry, is to see you doing something with your life. But I guess that's too much to ask."

I tried not to think about those words on my way into city centre. I stopped at a deli and ate with my eyes on the clock, as it was getting late in the afternoon and I wanted to make sure I was early for my meeting with the director of the Usual Company. I called there asking for Mr Holdwood, but got transferred to a man named Clive Louvagh, who said he was running the company. From what he'd told me in our phone call, he was open to talking about anything

32

that would help with the investigations. He was the one who used the i-word, but there was no way to hide it: I was investigating something. I just wasn't sure what.

On the radio, Angela had said she was positively sure that Lucy had triggered the alarm, but Lucy had had no way of doing that while standing in the middle of the auditorium. And judging by the way she'd been standing while the rest of the crowd was running, the alarm had been as much of a surprise for her as it was to everyone else. Sure, she could have been faking surprise, but for what? There wasn't anyone who was meant to see her in the middle of that mess.

And, thinking back, I realised that everyone seemed to have forgotten the words Lucy had spoken right before the alarm: "I want you to find the man who killed my father." Those words were the whole reason I'd set out on this investigation in the first place. Those words needed to be explained.

As it was nearly six, I headed to the Usual Company. I had a detective ID with me — in reality an old piece of memorabilia I'd bought a few years before. It had the name 'Lestrade' on it, but I figured if I showed it really quickly people wouldn't notice. Angela Dove didn't ask me for any identification, but I figured not everyone would be so naïve. I hoped that would do the trick.

The Usual Company was located in a hangar, on a street full of them. The doors were wide open, with a lot of people coming and going, most of them in costumes. I didn't feel the need to knock. A clown told me where I could find Mr Louvagh. His office door was open too, and as I entered, he was talking on the phone, a cigar in hand.

"I told you," he was saying, "the actor of the play within the play can't be more famous than the actor playing Hamlet." Pause. "It's pretty obvious to me!" Pause. "Okay, but it's like making a *Batman* movie where Robin's the bigger star. It just doesn't wash." He looked up and spotted me. "Okay, I got to go, call you later." He hung up and turned to me with a smile. "You must be Detective Bellamy."

I let him look at my fake ID for a second, and put it back in my pocket.

"Thank you so much for seeing me," I said, sitting across from him. "You seem to be very busy."

"An easy day is a wasted day, that's what I always say," he replied. "Want a cigar?"

I shook my head. "Thanks, but this shouldn't take long." I pulled the letter from my pocket and handed it to him. "Can you tell me something about this piece of paper? During the course of the investigation this letter emerged as evidence. I can't help but notice that the signature isn't yours."

He skimmed the letter. "You're right," he said, looking surprised. "It's been signed and stamped by Terence Holdwood."

"It's my understanding that you're the director of the Usual Company."

Louvagh sat back in his chair. "That's right. I took over when Terry died, four years ago."

"I see," I said. "Any idea how a man who's been dead four years could have signed and stamped a letter?"

Louvagh shook his head. "Anyone could have forged Terry's signature, though I don't know why they'd bother; anyone who's familiar with the company knows he's been gone for years. As far as the stamp goes…it got tossed a long time ago." He shrugged. "I suppose it might have been pulled from the bin, but if that's the case there's no way of knowing who's got it now." He regarded me thoughtfully. "What's all this about?"

As much as I liked Louvagh, I didn't want to tell him the whole story. It occurred to me that I probably should have thought this through beforehand, but never mind. Thinking quickly, I concocted a story about investigating a complaint a young woman had filed, saying she'd been told she'd been offered a role in the Usual Company only to find this wasn't the case.

"Oh, the brunette with the voice!" he said, surprising me with the quick recall. "Todd — Todd Smith, one of our directors — was the one who saw her. He said she thought she'd been offered a role in…"

"Who's Afraid of Virginia Woolf," I said.

"Yes, that one!" He shook his head. "We haven't done that play in at least twelve years. Are you telling me somebody tricked her into coming here?" He looked concerned as he added, "Somebody from our company?"

"I don't think so," I said. "If the woman who did this was from the Usual Company, I don't think she would have used its name. It would be easy to trace her back here. I do think, however, that she had some connection with the company — maybe something in her past? With so many theatre companies in London, she must have had a reason to choose yours."

"So," he said, "how can I help you?"

"Have you ever had a Lucy Ferguson in the company?"

He thought about it for a second.

"Nope. No Lucy Ferguson."

"Maybe her father."

"No, nobody named Ferguson. No need to consult the files; I have everyone single person that has ever been in the Usual Company right here," he said, tapping his forehead.

"She's petite. Ginger. Freckles. Nice body."

"I'd definitely remember that. Sorry, but your lady has never worked for us."

What to do next? I didn't have a plan B — I hadn't considered the possibility that the answer to my question would lead to a dead end. Which was embarrassing. I didn't seem so smart now, did I?

"Wait here a minute," he said, getting up and leaving the room. I sat and twiddled my thumbs for five minutes, hoping he'd come back with something good.

"Look at this picture," said Louvagh, handing it to me. It was an old black and white photo. Four actors were on the stage, two men and two women. The caption told me that it was a production still from *Who's Afraid of Virginia Woolf.* Louvagh pointed to the actor playing Nick. "This guy, Manny Randel."

"What about him?"

"The black and white hides it, but this guy is as ginger as it gets. This was the production I told you about, the one we did twelve years ago. He had a little daughter who was also training to be an actress. The reason I'm mentioning all this," he said, with a dramatic pause, "is that I read about his death in the papers, no more than a year ago. Murdered."

That was barely something. That could be the dead father Lucy Ferguson had mentioned, but Manny Randel could just as easily be a random redhead.

"The funny thing about Manny Randel," said Louvagh, "is that he later got a role on a TV show and had to dye his hair black and wear a fake black moustache."

"Really?" I said, interested. "What TV show?"

"Can't remember the name. I don't think he was on it for very long..."

Manny Randel. Manny Randel. That name was familiar, wasn't it? The more I thought about the name, the more familiar it sounded. Someone from the past. It was on the tip of my tongue, almost elementary...

"My dear Watson!" I said out loud.

The other night, when Caesar Ace was trying to show off at the convention, he'd mentioned that most people believed there were three actors who'd played Watson in the show. He also mentioned that one of the episodes was originally aired with a different actor in the role, and then reshot. That made four Watsons. But I knew that show better than anyone. There was a fifth Watson. An actor who served as a double to Neville's original co-star, Marky Duvall,

37

during the shooting of *The Hound of the Baskervilles*. They had an uncanny resemblance, and only someone who watched the episode a thousand times (and I did) would spot the difference. This double's name wasn't credited with the rest of the cast, but there was a name that was thanked in the closing credits. The name was Manny Randel.

CHAPTER FOUR

Jar of Pennies

I drove around for a couple of hours, burning a lot of petrol trying to make something out of that. I wouldn't have the money to fill the tank before bringing it back to Pete, but it didn't matter. Things were getting confusing. Was there something behind Lucy's appearance at the convention, or was just a weird coincidence? Maybe it was more than that. Or maybe it was nothing. She could be friends with Neville; after all, he and her father had worked together for some time.

You had to be a true *The Baker Street Sleuth* aficionado in order to spot the five Watsons. All the actors looked a lot alike. Manny Randel had doubled Marky Duvall in only two scenes, and according to Louvagh, the makers made him dye his hair in order not to look any different from him.

The thing was, Lucy came to Neville for help. Her father was dead, and she wanted Neville to investigate it. It could very well be another hoax. After all, Angela Dove was at the auditorium that same night, and her only job was to make Neville look smart.

Things like that don't just happen. They got to have a meaning. Once when I was fourteen, this kid from the neighbourhood came to me for help. He lost the jar of pennies he kept in his bedroom and wanted me to investigate it. I was just a kid who watched too much TV, but he trusted me the same way Lucy seemed to trust Neville. I came back home to get rubber gloves, baby powder to identify fingerprints. I was so excited by my first case! After this one was solved, I figured the other kids would want me to solve their mysteries, and then, who knew what could happen? Fame? Glory? All that went down the drain when I got to my friend's home and he told me his mother had found the jar of pennies. I went back home with my gloves and my baby powder and sat on the bed feeling very frustrated.

It may sound absurd, but I was feeling the exact same way about that case — if it could even be called that. I could feel that jar of pennies being found; I could feel my chance of doing something being taken away from me again. The situation was very odd, and I knew the right thing to do was to go back home and forget it all. I was probably just chasing windmills. Playing detective had been fun for a while, especially with so many people buying my story, but now it was time to go back to the real world. A world where I was a nobody.

I stopped the car in front of my building, but didn't get out. What if there was something else? What if I was throwing the chance of my life by letting that go too fast? "Think, Jerry!" I said to myself. "Think, for Christ's sake!"

Okay. I had a girl with a dead father. An actor who played a detective. Somebody who didn't want her to finish her saying. How to put it all together? Maybe a piece of that puzzle was missing. What could it be? I thought it over and over, trying to make something out of it. There had to be something there.

But all I had were pieces that didn't fit each other. It was so much easier for the guys who wrote TV shows! For them, if a piece was missing, it was only a matter of changing the final picture. Add a little something there, and it'll make sense. I was no Sherlock Holmes, but I could find a way of solving that mystery if only I allowed myself to be a little creative. Just a little. It wouldn't be cheating — that is, if anyone can actually cheat reality — but just a shortcut to the truth. After I got there, I would go back and find the way that led to that truth. "Nothing too much," I said to myself. "Just a little something to make things go smoother."

Let's think about it. Maybe Manny Randel found some secret in Neville's past and was killed for it. But that would make Neville more of a suspect than a possible investigator. It didn't make sense. Well, maybe Neville was the one who knew something about Manny Randel, and in that secret lay the reason of his murder. But what secret could it be? No, that was too much speculation. What about this: Lucy was actually the one who killed her father, and was trying to distract the police by putting Neville in that investigation. Yes, that was good!

It might be good, alright, but not juicy enough. I needed to make up a better story. Was 'making up' a bad choice of words? I tried to believe I was doing something else. After all, I wasn't creating evidence and leads out of nowhere — was I? Real life deduction wasn't that easy. I was trying to cut to the chase, imagine the end of the road to make the walk easier.

But I needed a better end to that line of thought. Something that could really shake people up. First I had to create it. Then, make it real.

"Think, Jerry! What if this was a TV episode and you were trying to surprise everyone? What would you use? You already have murder. But how to make murder even better?"

Something popped out from my mind. Something good. What about a serial killer? They always sell, don't they? But this serial killer had something different in mind. I couldn't avoid smiling when I figured out which angle to take. It was something so smart I could write a whole book out of it.

But I couldn't go to the police with something like that. I could try to find Lucy and tell her what I knew. Granted, I didn't really know anything, but had a really good guess, and even though I had no proof, she was a pretty good lead. Now I just had to back it up with facts. The story had to be believable. After all, if it was believable, it would be true.

I went to the nearest pub, sat by the counter and ordered a pint. There was still some work to be done before bringing my theories to the public. I borrowed a pen from the barman and wrote everything I already had on a napkin.

So I already had a case in my hands. Or at the very least, the idea of a case. Now I had to put that idea in the real world. It was all related to *The Baker Street Sleuth* and the actors who had portrayed Watson. I made a diagram of the seasons and any information that could be useful. I had already filled seven napkins and not even touched my beer when an old familiar tune came to my ears. It was the opening theme of *The Baker Street Sleuth*. I used to watch that rerun at work. Damn, I should have been at work a long time ago! Well, that bridge was most likely burned now, so I might as well have a pint and watch the show.

It was one of the late episodes, after the series had gotten mediocre. Some idiot decided that Irene Adler should come back to London declaring she was expecting Holmes' son. It was a scheme, as it used to be, but not a very good one. Of course Holmes finds out what she's up to, something involving a missing jewel, and in the end everything goes back to its right place. I once watched that episode with Andrea Linskey by my side. Better not to think about

42

her, I guess. She made it very clear how pathetic she thought I was. Anyway, if I were really creating that whole picture with the serial killer I wanted to catch, it might be better to create a love interest for me. What about that ginger girl at the auditorium, Lucy Ferguson? She seemed like the kind of girl that would fall in love for the detective in some cheesy mystery novel.

The episode was about to end and I was getting ready to go home when the guy sitting next to me pointed at the screen and said, "Hey, I've been to this guy's neighbourhood, a couple of months ago!"

I looked at the owner of that voice. He was about thirty-five years old, dressed in a blue plaid shirt, dirty jeans and a grey cap. His hands were rough and had paint splatters all over them. Not the kind of person who's acquainted with celebrities. "You mean you know him?" I asked. "You know Sir Bartholomew Neville?"

"I never said I knew him," he said, pleased to show he had met a famous person. "I was painting a house and went to the street to smoke a cigarette when I saw the guy walking uphill with his groceries."

"Groceries?" I asked. "You mean a bag of groceries?"

"Yes," he said. "Brown paper bag. Oranges, bread, milk. Why are you so interested?"

"I'm sorry," I said, smiling at him. "Why don't you let me buy you a pint?"

The barman brought him a glass of dark beer. He asked me if I wanted anything, but I said no. I still intended to drive that night.

43

"So," I said. "You are a house painter."

"Yep!" said the man and then he burped. "Tough job. Not for everyone."

"Are you sure you saw that man on the TV?" I asked very slowly.

"No doubt!" he said, drinking his pint. "I never forget a face."

"Was he on foot?" I asked. "This is very important. Was he on foot?"

"Why is this so important?" He stared at me, and for the first time there was suspicion in his face. I wasn't going to say it, but if Neville was on foot, that could mean he lived in the neighbourhood where that man saw him. It could also mean he was walking to his car, and in that case he could live anywhere else. But I wasn't going to throw away that lead so easily.

I changed the question. "Would you be able to tell me where that was?"

"Why should I tell you?" he asked, and I could see the guy was about to walk away. I smiled at him again.

"Your glass is almost empty," I said. "Why don't we get you a refill?"

It took me two more pints to make him open his mouth. He finally told me everything. He was painting the front door of a house when he looked back and recognised the face of the old man walking uphill with his groceries. At first he thought of asking for an autograph, but his hands and clothes were covered in paint and he didn't think that was a good idea to approach such an important person in those conditions.

"Have you seen him after that?" I asked.

"No, I haven't!" he said, with the smile of someone who has drunk too much. "But let me tell, you my friend, of one time when me and my girl..."

"The address," I said, and wasn't smiling anymore. "What's the address?"

"I don't remember!" he said. "I think I remember the name of the street..." He gave it a little thought and then told me the name he remembered. "But now let me tell you another story..."

"I got more important things to do," I said, getting up and going away without paying for his drink. I now had something to start with.

CHAPTER FIVE

No Baker Street

It was already pitch black when I found the house. I had knocked on many doors, asking for information, until someone was able to tell me were Sir Bartholomew lived. It was a very nice neighbourhood; the trees didn't have messages carved on them and the people who walked around with their dogs always carried a small bag to collect the poop. But it was no Baker Street, and not the least bit glamorous. Definitely not as I imagined.

I took a deep breath and knocked on his door. How many times had I imagined myself doing that? Standing in front of my greatest hero's front door, expecting him to come and answer! To be perfectly honest, that was so fantastic I had never even dared to fantasise it.

Too bad I wasn't there to smile at him and say how much I loved his work. I was there to present a theory of a murder — in fact, a series of murders. And as I stood by that door, the whole thing started to sound a little silly. After all, I had zero evidence about what happened — hell, I couldn't even prove it did happen. Prudence would've told me to turn my back to that door and go away. But instead, I knocked again.

I knew my chances of finding Neville at this hour were minimal. At this time of night he was likely rehearsing a play, shooting a new movie or appearing at another convention. If the rumours were true, he'd be flying to Romania, learning his lines to play Abraham van Helsing. I told myself that if he wasn't at home, the best thing would be to forget the whole thing right there and return to my regular, boring life. Just the fact I was there was weird enough, and I knew I could get into trouble. But I knocked a third time, trying to look as serious as possible. Worst case scenario, I'd know where to send my fan mail directly. If he did open the door, that meant I was about to realise the dream of a lifetime. But if he was there, I had to look professional. My heart was pumping like crazy and my legs were shaking; I kept telling them to put themselves together and help me out with my act.

The door hinges creaked, sounding similar to Angela Dove's voice. An old Guy Lombardo song came from inside the house. Bartholomew Neville had opened the door and was looking at me.

"May I help you?" he asked.

Man, he was old! So much older than he'd appeared to be less than a day ago! It was him, all right. That bent back and those tired eyes didn't conceal the greatness of the man, but he wasn't playing Sherlock Holmes now. That wasn't an act.

I spoke.

"Sir Bartholomew, my name is Jerry Bellamy and I…" The whole speech had been carefully rehearsed, but now my mouth was trembling, and I couldn't complete the sentence. "I'm a fan!" I finally said, and instantly regretted it. I was supposed to be a detective, not a fan!

Neville seemed very bored by my presence. "Just a second," he said and went back inside. I stood there. Two minutes later he was back, with two different photographs in his hands.

"Look, I got a picture from series one, with Natasha Richardson as Irene Adler, for fifteen pounds, and another from series three, with

47

Jay Mortigan as Moriarty. This one is already signed for another person, so I'll make a nice price for you."

"Sir Bartholomew, I…I'm not here to buy an autograph." I should probably get to the point as soon as possible, but the whole situation was so unreal I couldn't make sense out of my own words.

He took off his glasses and examined me with pale green eyes. They didn't seem so sharp and wise now. They were just an old man's eyes.

"Please don't tell me you have a fanzine. I don't give interviews to that kind of…"

"Sir Bartholomew, I'm here to save your life," I finally said.

That phrase didn't have the impact I expected. Neville didn't seem a bit surprised. It was like he was used to hearing those words.

"Goodnight, son," he said, looking tired. "If I die you can come by my funeral and say you warned me."

He put the photos in his pocket and was about to shut the door when I reached out with my hand.

"Please, Sir Bartholomew, you've got to hear me."

"You know what, I don't," he said. "Look, I'm an old man. I love my fans, but sometimes you all love me a little too much."

"There's a killer going around, and he's killing the Watsons."

Neville stopped trying to close the door; I'd got his attention. I couldn't tell how long I'd be able to keep it, so I quickly shoved the newspaper clippings at him that I had photocopied at the public library before coming to him.

"Do you remember Marky Duvall?" I asked.

He put his glasses back on and read the obituary I had marked in red. That was on the top of the clippings.

"It says here he was found dead two months ago," Neville said, "but the name doesn't ring any bells."

Well, that was oddly disappointing. "He was your first Watson," I said. "In the first series of *The Baker Street Sleuth*. He has been murdered, and I don't believe it was by chance."

Neville scratched his head, trying his best to remember Duvall. I didn't blame him. With so many different Watsons on that show, you'd think at least one of them would be memorable, but that wasn't the case.

"I don't follow you," said Neville. He consulted the obituary again. "Says here he was killed by a burglar. What makes you think it was premeditated murder? And even if it was, why did you come to me in the first place?"

"Last night," I said, "at the convention. There was a redhead in the middle row who asked for your help finding her father's killer. Remember?"

Neville frowned. "Yes," he said. "She seemed familiar at the time."

"I'm almost completely sure she was the daughter of Manny Randel. Randel served as a double to Watson in *The Hound of the Baskervilles*."

He was looking me in the eyes now. "Really?" he said. I nodded. "I've heard a lot of crazy things in my time, but nothing like this. Either you're pulling a really well-rehearsed act, or you're on to something."

"Can I come inside?" I asked. "I want to discuss it with you."

He stared at me for a long time. Of course he wouldn't let me in! He'd have to be crazy to do so. I was prepared for a rejection, but then I realised there was some sort of glow in his eyes. Like he was happy that I had come by.

"I don't think this is wise of me," he said with a quirky smile. He hesitated, and then added, "Guess you look harmless enough. Might as well come in and have a cup of tea." He stood back and held open the door. I held my breath and entered.

The interior of Neville's house was a true Sherlock Holmes Museum. His walls were covered with illustrations, movie posters, photographs and other memorabilia. He had a shelf with at least ten editions of each one of Sir Arthur Conan Doyle's novels and another one with what seemed like a million VHS tapes of the different Sherlock Holmes movies and TV series. To a fan like me, walking into the kitchen was like walking into Disneyworld. But the greatest thing of all was a full size sculpture of Neville himself, dressed as the sleuth. The real one seemed even smaller by its side, though they still were the same size.

"So, Mr Bellamy," he said, setting the kettle to boil. "You mentioned Manny Randel. Do you have any proof he's also been murdered?"

"I couldn't find anything in the papers," I said. "All I have is Lucy Ferguson asking for your help."

"Ms Ferguson," he said. "Quite a beauty, huh? Now that you've mentioned it, I remember a little redheaded girl tagging along after Randel on set, always wearing a pretty dress and pigtails. But not a lot to go on if you're going to go around declaring you've found a serial killer..."

"There is another thing."

"I'm all ears."

"It's come to my attention that the guy at the convention with the *Tomorrow Never Dies* t-shirt was, well... staged," I said.

Neville served the tea.

"That isn't something I'm proud of," he said. "but it helps sell tickets. You see, most people still think that Holmes and I are the same person."

"I know that," I said, "and I also know that you're not Holmes, in case you're wondering if I've made the same mistake. Lucy Ferguson also knows that, especially given her dad was one of your Watsons." I paused for effect, and then said, "So the question is: why did Lucy Ferguson come to you for help? She knows you're not a real detective, so why come to you? I'm betting she thinks you know something that can help her find the killer."

"Assuming there is a killer, of course."

"Of course." I sighed and then confessed, "And that's all I got."

Neville thought for several minutes. I drank my tea without saying a word. Finally he spoke.

"I'm about to tell you something that really ought to be kept confidential. I probably shouldn't tell you, since best case scenario you're trying to get a story and worse case you're the killer you've been telling me about." He looked at me and a smile crept over his face. "Let's just assume you're neither." He sighed. "The thing is, in the last four months or so I've been receiving some weird fan mail. Hate mail. It's not so uncommon for a famous person to get this kind of this kind of thing, so I actually didn't think they were important until now. I would have gone to the police otherwise. You made me a bit worried."

"Do you have these letters now?"

"With me? No. My agent has them."

"And what did they say?"

"Death threats, erotic drawings, all the good stuff." He finished his tea and got up. "I'll go upstairs and I'll call my agent. I'll also ask if he's heard anything about the other Watsons, or if he can help me make contact with them. Please make yourself at home."

He went, leaving me alone in the kitchen. Once I heard his footsteps going upstairs, I decided to explore a little. His living room was a fanboy's wet dream. It was impossible to examine every single piece of memorabilia in the short time I had, so I went straight to the objects that Neville had used in the original series. There were four mannequin heads, each one covered with fake eyebrows, fake moustaches and fake noses: the many disguises Holmes wore in his investigations. Under a protection glass I found laboratory flasks used in the amazing experiments conducted at Baker Street 221B. There was even a place for the cane Dr Mortimer forgot with Mrs Hudson in *The Hound of the Baskervilles*. It was lying over a small table, and I had to exercise real restraint not to touch any of his stuff.

Suddenly I heard a scream, followed by the sound of something heavy falling to the ground. It had come from upstairs, and I realised, my heart in my mouth, that it was Neville who'd screamed. I ran up the stairs as fast as I could and practically kicked the door open. Neville was on the ground, a bust of Athena by his side. Taking in the situation at a glance, I came to the conclusion that someone had tried to hit him over the head with the bust, but had missed and hit him in the shoulder instead.

"Over there!" he said, pointing. "He escaped through the window."

I looked out the window at a large concrete terrace, completely empty except for a small barbecue grill in the corner. The window was at least twelve feet above ground; it was possible somebody could have jumped down to the courtyard, run very fast and then jumped the back wall. It was, but at that moment I didn't have time to think about it. Neville needed my help.

"Are you okay?" I asked, moving back to his side.

"I'll be fine," he said. "A tall man with a mask was here, like he was waiting for me all the time," he said, getting to his feet. "You can put that down now."

I looked down and realised I held the cane in my hand. I must have grabbed it in the heat of the moment.

"It could be worse," he said, nudging the bust with his foot. "It could be a hell of a lot worse."

Neville sat down, resting his chin on his hands; I could see the gears in his head slowly start moving as he tried thinking of something.

"I made those phone calls," he said at last, backtracking a bit. "My agent is trying to contact the other Watsons. Right now I think we should call the police. Now please, I could use some sherry. Do you mind opening me a bottle?"

Drinking sherry with Bartholomew Neville? I felt tempted to pinch myself to confirm it wasn't a dream, but the moment required me to get a grip on myself. After a couple of glasses we called the police and he decided to open a bottle of scotch in order to cool our heads while we waited for the cops to arrive.

CHAPTER SIX

The Ginger Girl

By the time I finished answering the questions the cops asked me, I'd burned a lot of bridges. I was officially fired from the quick market and I was officially involved in that investigation. And I had lied to the cops about how I'd ended up in Bartholomew Neville's house. He made up some crazy story about being my uncle and that I was just paying him a visit. I wasn't sure why we were lying. Neville just started talking and I went along with him. It was really dumb, but it actually was quite exciting, too. I could tell he wanted that case and somehow wanted me to be by his side. So I just said yes to all his questions. Everything that had happened, the fire alarm, the murder theories, even the killer attacking Neville in his house while I was downstairs — it was all, in a weird way, everything I could ever want to happen. I didn't understand it, but I wouldn't let it go away.

Neville and I weren't able to talk in private again for the rest of that night. They insisted on bringing Neville to hospital, so we decided to meet the following day for lunch. I took my brother's car and drove home. The keys to my flat were in my hand when I went upstairs and saw somebody sitting outside my front door.

"Good evening," she said.

The ginger girl was waiting for me. I stared at her for a while, quite shocked, to be honest. "Lucy, isn't that right?" I said, playing with the keys in my hand. "How did you know where I live?"

"I followed you," she said, standing up. "You're an easy guy to follow. I thought you'd never finish parking that car."

"The car is kinda big," I said

"What's your name?" she asked.

"You followed me without knowing my name?" I asked. She stared at me without replying.

Lucy's beautiful copper hair was loose around her shoulders. She wore a black top and tight black trousers, and for the first time I was able to admire her body, though it was better not to. She looked at me with blue eyes and I soon realised she was more dangerous than Neville's attacker. "My name is Jerry."

"Can I come inside with you?"

I stared at her, thinking about that request. "Is this something you do on a regular basis? Following guys you don't know around, coming to their houses and asking to come inside?"

"I've never done this before," she said. "None of this."

She was challenging me, and I was completely lost. 'Play the detective!' an irritating voice at the back of my head yelled. "So why should you trust me?" I asked, and added after a few seconds, "Or why should I trust you?"

She took something out of her purse. A small plastic device with a big red button. "See this? I pay for my own protection," she said, pretending to press the button. "I bought this after my dad was killed. It wasn't cheap, but it's very useful. If I push this button, this place will be full of cops in two minutes."

"I don't think that's how it works," I said.

"I can press the button and we'll see," she said. "Or we can go inside and talk."

"And how is this any safer for me?" I asked, my eyes on the button.

"It is your place, isn't it?" Lucy answered, putting the device in her trouser pocket. "And I don't think you'll be able to sleep tonight without hearing what I have to say."

"What's the worst that can happen?" I asked, reaching past her to put the key in the lock. "Guess if you kill me, my life expectancy bottoms out, but at least it'll be an interesting final few minutes. That's good enough for me." I pushed the door open, too tired and too confused to make better sense. "Make yourself comfortable," I said as we entered my little flat.

She threw herself on the couch. "Can I bother you for a cup of coffee?"

"Sure" I said, going to the kitchen. Lucy seemed really comfortable for someone who had never done this before. She was looking around at my flat like she was trying to evaluate what kind of life I had.

"How did you get into all of this?" she asked me.

"I was at the convention," I said. "I heard you asking Neville about your father."

"I see," she said. "Are you one of those fanboys?"

"I guess so," I said. "You didn't answer my question."

Lucy got up and started to look at my collection of VHS tapes. "Jeez, you really are into this, aren't you? I see a lot of TV stuff, but no original Sherlock Holmes books at all. Wait a minute, what's this?" I ran to the living room, and she had a VHS box in her right hand and the panic device in her left. She hadn't pushed it, at least not yet. "*The Baker Street Slut?*" she said. "You have a copy of a Sherlock Holmes porno?"

"It's part of my collection," I said. "It's a very rare tape."

"It's creepy as hell," she said. "You not a pervert, are you?"

I took it out of her hand and put it back on the shelf. "Coffee is ready," I said. "Could you answer my question? How did you find me?"

"I stopped by to see Neville. The cops were there, so I parked on the corner and waited for three hours until they went away."

"Why didn't you come into the house instead of following me?" I looked up at her. "Cream and sugar?"

"Cream, no sugar." She shrugged. "I wanted to see if you knew about him. The Watson killer."

My cup almost fell out of my hand when she said that. "So is it true?" I asked.

"Of course it's true," Lucy said. "Are you going after him?"

I was so happy I almost didn't hear her. So my deduction (if you can call it that) was right! There was a killer going around, and I was one of the few people who knew it.

"Jerry!" she said, snapping her fingers in front of my face. "Is there anyone in there?"

"I'm here," I said. "Are you saying the killer is real?"

"I can assure you of that," she said. "Are you going after him?"

Was I? That was a great question, and I had no idea how to answer it. Going from bagger at a quick market to a serial killer hunter was a pretty big jump, and I wasn't sure if I could do it. But the jar of pennies came back to my mind. If I didn't grab it that time, it might never come again.

"I'm in," I said. "I'm on the hunt."

"Did you see the tall man?" she asked.

"No, but Neville did. Is he the killer?"

"I'm not sure," she said. "But he's our best suspect. I don't even have his name, though. Tell me what you know."

I told her everything, from the beginning. When I was finished, she told me her part of the story.

"My real name is Catherine Brown. Lucy Ferguson is my stage name, and it's what I prefer to go by. Dad was on *The Baker Street Sleuth* in 1991. The casting agent thought he looked a bit like the previous Watson. After he dyed his hair and grew a moustache, they were dead ringers. Papa didn't care much for TV, but the money was good, so he took it."

I went to the kitchen to fix myself another cup of coffee. She seemed a bit too excited by that story, like she was happy her father died, just so she could come at a stranger's flat and tell it.

"Your father was very good in the role," I said. It was a silly compliment, since her father hadn't been more than a body double, but I felt like saying something.

"He didn't care much for their show," Lucy said. "Neville was a pompous ass and made the lives of everyone on set really difficult. When they were filming, Dad spent most of his time in his room, rehearsing monologues he hoped to do on the stage after the series ended. At the end of the season, he quit of his own free will; that pissed Neville off, because he wanted to be the one controlling when and how people came and went on the series. I'm afraid your beloved idol vowed that my father would never again be able to find work in London — and he made it happen."

I wasn't sure if I believed her. But then again, nothing about Neville seemed to be certain anymore. I just nodded and let her finish her story.

"Time went by, but Dad never got a good role again. And that's a shame, because he was such a good actor, more than anybody else on the show. He had so many talents, but Neville made it so he couldn't ever use them. He worked as a cab driver for his remaining years and taught me the principles of acting. I was supposed to take his place, and succeed where he couldn't."

"And did you?" I asked.

"Working on backstage now," she said, sipping her coffee. "It's easier, though less rewarding, but —" she shrugged "— one can't be picky. I don't have lots of awards, but that's okay. Dad had a chance to be proud of me before he was murdered last year." She stared down into her cup for a moment, and then said, "A passenger shot him three times from the back seat of his cab. The police said it was a robbery gone wrong, and for a while I believed that. It made sense. Then, while cleaning his car, I found this."

Lucy dug into her handbag and handed me a piece of paper. It had the numbers one to five written out, and the first two were scratched off.

"At first I couldn't figure out what it meant," Lucy said. "But then I realised that the line across number two is shaky, and the paper is very creased right over that same number. You surely know what that means."

I had absolutely no clue of what that could mean, but didn't want to tell her that. Thankfully, Lucy kept talking.

"It's like somebody scratched out the word in a moving vehicle, using his lap as a desk. In other words, he marked my father's name on the list, killed him and forgot his killing list on the back seat. My father was Watson number two."

"That's pretty flimsy evidence," I said.

"I know. And I didn't think much about it," Lucy said, "until I found out that Marky Duvall had also been murdered in his house by a burglar. I talked to Duvall's daughter and she said her dad was shot three times in the back while trying to defend his home. Three times the back," she repeated. "Just like my dad."

"Hmm…" I moaned, trying to think of something smart to say. I was playing a detective, after all. Too bad I didn't have the skills of Holmes, the calmness of Maigret or the cynicism of Sam Spade. That didn't leave much for me. Maybe it was time to get help. "I think we should call Neville right away!"

She stared at me, disappointed. That wasn't such a smart thing to say after all.

"I think I had the wrong idea about you," she said. "I mean, if you can't see it…"

"What?" I asked. "What am I supposed to see?"

Lucy knew something I didn't, or, worse, she saw something that I didn't. Something I either couldn't realise…or wasn't willing to realise. So I cleared my mind and thought back to the start. If I expanded my suspect pool to include anyone and everyone, and I was the only person I could trust… It suddenly became clear.

"You think Neville is the killer!" I said.

"Are you seriously telling me you never thought about that possibility?" she asked, angry. "It should've been the first thing to pop into your mind!"

She was right. I felt like a child who reads his first mystery novel and can't see the clues that are right in front of him. Neville had definitely faked that attack. He could have thrown the bust on the floor and pretended to have been hit. Now that I thought about it, he didn't even show that wound to the cops.

"Here's what I've come up with," she said. "Neville was caught in the middle of something. Maybe he's done something illegal or that he's ashamed of. Someone is blackmailing him, but he doesn't know who. Somehow he finds out that his blackmailer is a Watson. A Watson!"

"And how the hell does that work?" I asked.

"I don't know, but just listen," she said. "So, he can't find out which Watson did it, so he decides to kill them one by one, starting with the first. The trick is that he has to do it so that the blackmailer doesn't realise Neville is hunting the Watsons down."

"Oh my God!" I said. "That's why you were at that convention! You wanted to expose him!"

"I know I don't have much," she said. "But I wanted to draw attention to the murders. There was some press there, and the papers love that kind of stuff. Imagine the morning news: someone is killing Watsons and Sherlock Holmes is on the case. Suddenly everyone would know about the case, including the blackmailer. And whatever Neville is hiding wouldn't be a secret for much longer."

"I have an appointment tomorrow," I said suddenly, coffee pot in hand. "A lunch with Neville. I don't know what to do anymore."

"You should go," she said. "I'll be around."

"Listen, Lucy," I tried to speak as calmly as possible. "Your story makes some sense, but I don't know if I can help you."

"What do you mean?" she asked, confused. "I'm here, I told you my story. You got to help me."

"Please, just listen," I said. "When I woke up this morning, my life was very simple. I didn't like it, but at least I could make some sense out of it."

She got up slowly, looking at me with a serious face. "I really took you the wrong way."

"I guess you did," I said. "Now I need you to go. I really do."

A sad smile came to her face. She stared at the floor for a few seconds, than stared at me again. "I wish I didn't have to do this," she said.

"Do what?" I asked.

Lucy showed me her empty cup again. "Can I have another one? Then I'll be gone."

"The pot is empty," I said.

"Then I guess you'll have to make more coffee."

I went back to the kitchen and filled the pot with water. I expected Lucy to keep talking, but she didn't utter a word while I made the coffee. I filled her cup and went back to the living room, but stopped as soon as I got to the door. Lucy was there, with that sad smile and tired eyes. She was completely naked.

"Lucy, you don't have to do this," I said.

She walked in my direction, took the cup out of my hand and put it on the floor. "I'm afraid I do," she said, kissing my face. "Where is your room?" I pointed the direction. Lucy grabbed me by the hand and led me to my bedroom. And here I thought things couldn't get any more confusing. Didn't fight it, though. Nerdy guy goes to bed with hot-blooded redhead who doesn't seem to want strings attached. My dreams were all coming true, in a creepy way.

CHAPTER SEVEN

Bed and Breakfast

The smell of bacon and eggs woke me up from a series of bizarre dreams. It wasn't until I realised that I wasn't wearing any clothes that the events of the previous night came back to me. Lucy was still in my flat, and apparently making breakfast.

"Good morning," she said as I came into the kitchen. "You really need groceries."

A woman in her knickers and wearing a man's crumpled t-shirt is a million times sexier than any fashion model in a bikini. Unfortunately for me, my enjoyment of Lucy's long legs was marred by the fact that she was dragging me along on her vendetta. Kind of hard to escape the reminder, seeing as the t-shirt she was wearing had Neville's Holmes plastered across it.

"I'll steal some food later," I said, helping myself to a cup of coffee. "How did you sleep?"

"Just fine." Lucy smiled at me. "You got me tired."

Breakfast looked delicious, and I attacked it without mercy. The eggs were spectacular.

"Your brother called, by the way," she said, lighting a cigarette. "He wanted his car back, and seemed a bit surprised by me answering the phone."

"Damn, I forgot about the car!"

"He seemed nice," she said. "Wish I had a brother or a sister. Life wouldn't be so tough."

"Do you have any family left, Lucy?" I asked around a mouthful of eggs. "Anyone that cares about you?"

"I have a few friends," she said. "Not many, though. People don't usually like me. Anyway, where are you meeting Neville?"

"I'm not sure about bringing you with me," I said.

"Why not?" she asked, crushing the cigarette on a saucer. I expected her to be more upset. "You know I'm going to follow you anyway. What do you think I'll do, kill him in front of everyone?"

I put the eggs aside. "Then what exactly do you plan to do, Lucy? Is this a revenge tale, or what?"

She fixed herself a cup of coffee and leaned against the wall. "I'm not sure. But I can't simply sit back and do nothing."

I started to think about how weird the whole situation was. But I was a smart guy, wasn't I? I mean, I had predicted the whole thing about the killer, and that seemed to work. Maybe I should trust my instincts, and they were telling me to give Lucy some help.

"Juliano's Brazilian Food," I said. "We're supposed to meet there at eleven o'clock."

"And what are you going to talk about?"

"I'm hoping that Neville has material on the other Watsons. He said last night he'd made some calls. I'm guessing he'll probably have some information on you, so he can't know we know each other, obviously, or about…whatever this is."

66

"Guilty sex?!" she said, grinning.

"Let's call it a partnership," I replied. "Partnership covers all manner of sins. What are you going to do while I'm out with Neville?"

"I'll sit close to you. I won't be able to hear you, but I'll be able to see you. If I need to talk to you, I'll light a cigarette."

"What would you need me for?" I asked.

"Anything can help," Lucy answered. "And I'm really good at reading body language, so it'll be pretty obvious if you're betraying our agreement."

"And just what was that agreement again?" I asked, not bothering to hide the sarcasm. "I don't think I heard it the first time."

She put her hands on her hips and stared me down. "You help me bring Neville down and expose him to the world, letting my dad finally get the rest he deserves."

"And what do I get in exchange?" I asked. "Or am I meant to do this out of the goodness of my heart?"

"What do you want?" she asked. "Money? Because that's something I really can't offer."

I wasn't really sure what kind of services I was about to provide, therefore it wouldn't be easy to give her a price. Lucy stared at me, expecting me to say something. I stared at my clock and saw a great chance to change subjects. "We have two hours before I have to leave." I moved into the living room. "Can I show you something?"

I had most episodes of *The Baker Street Sleuth* on VHS. "You must have seen this episode before," I said, putting the tape in the VCR. "It's about a family hunted by the spectre of a supernatural dog."

"I saw as a child," she said. "Dad had bad memories of this show, so I never bothered watching it again."

On the screen, Watson was walking side by side with Henry Baskerville. It was hard to imagine there were two different actors playing the doctor throughout those shots. But I knew it and so did Lucy. The footage was old, but it had the desired effect. She watched the TV and I watched her eyes. They were shining. A reluctant smile appeared on her lips before fading away, and she turned her head from the screen.

"I don't want to see any more," she said. "I'd rather not..."

Her voice trailed off, so she ran to the bedroom and started putting on makeup. I rewound the tape and decided it was time for me to start getting ready for lunch, too.

CHAPTER EIGHT

The Jigsaw Crockery Routine

Lucy chose a table a good distance from me. I chose a table at the back of the restaurant and ordered a salad while waiting for Neville. Soon he arrived, looking very different from both the world's greatest detective and the celebrity caught in the privacy of his own home. Was I the only one not playing a character? Maybe it was time to start.

"Hope I didn't keep you waiting," said Neville. "Couldn't find the place."

He seemed oddly joyful for a man who could be in danger, dressed in a green coat with leather elbow patches and carrying an old brief bag. He seemed pleased to join me, bearing a great deal of new information.

"I'll have a plate of cattlemen beans," he said after examining the menu. Once the waiter had gone away, Neville opened the brief bag. "Lots to talk about, young man. Let's start with these."

He took his infamous hate mail out of an envelope. They were written in letters cut out from magazines and were mostly generic threats like "Your day is coming!", "Enjoy success while you can have it!", "Last season for you" and similar ratings. There were also many weird drawings of Sherlock Holmes in awkward sexual positions. According to Neville, he had received about twenty of these in his fan mail in the previous four months, all in the same kind of pink envelope.

"What do you think?" he asked.

I riffled through the letters. "These mean nothing."

"What do you mean?" He seemed a little upset.

"I don't think there's a single celebrity out there who hasn't received a letter like this at some point. And to be fair, our guy..."

"Girl."

"Sorry?"

"Lucy Ferguson is the one that's been killing men. It's her," he said. "She's the Watson Killer."

The girl at the next table continued drinking her coke, all alone at her table. Had she heard Neville? If she had, what would she do next? My eyes lingered on her for five seconds, almost betraying her location. Thankfully, Neville didn't seem to notice it. He was too excited by his own discoveries.

"Think about this for a second," he said, spreading five pictures across the table. "This is Marky Duvall. This is Manny Randel. And these are our next Watsons." He accompanied each name with a jab of his finger. "None of these last three have done much work in show business since leaving *The Baker Street Sleuth*, so my agent asked for a few more days to find information on them. But we won't need it."

"I don't follow you," I said. "If she isn't seeking revenge for Manny Randel..."

"The vengeful daughter is an old cliché, my friend," he said. "This case is actually quite simple."

"Wait a minute!" I said. "Let me see if I follow you. Do you mean she isn't Randel's daughter?"

"She is his daughter!" Neville said, almost shouting. He took a deep breath and, when he spoke again, he was quieter. "Or at least she's become his daughter. That's the beauty of it! Have you ever heard of the jigsaw crockery routine?"

"Sure I have!"

I'd read about the jigsaw crockery routine in any number of mysteries. Let's say you want to steal a china plate that's worth a million dollars from a cupboard filled with other plates, which together are worth just half a million. You plan to steal the plate you want from the cupboard — but how to avoid getting caught? You break the rest of the plates, leaving the pieces on the floor. If they're tiny enough, nobody will ever be able to tell there's a plate missing.

When it comes to murder, it's the same principle. You want a person dead, but don't want the cops to suspect you. You are the prime suspect for a rational murder, but the jigsaw crockery routine is all about preventing the cops from looking for a person with motive. You go around and kill a few other people with the same weapon you used for the murder you actually wanted to commit; the cops will assume that the crimes are the product of a deranged lunatic committing a series of crazy murders. They won't look for a reasonable killer anymore; they'll go after a crazy serial killer. And if you don't fit the serial killer profile, the police won't ever think of you again. It's as brilliant as it is perverse.

"So you think Lucy wanted to kill her dad and used the jigsaw crockery routine to fool everyone?" I asked.

Coming to think about it, it could make sense if she had a motive. In a way, it made even more sense than the idea that Neville was being blackmailed so he had to kill all the Watsons just to get rid of one. The only question was why...

"Why would she do it?" I asked, turning the question to Neville for consideration. "Why kill her own father?"

"What reasons could anyone have to kill a parent?" He sighed. "At first it all seemed too blurry, but then I realised Lucy might not be quite who she says she is. Tell me, how do we know she's actually Manny Randel's daughter?"

"But didn't you say?"

"I'm not talking about the man, Manny Randel. The name, boy. I'm talking about the name!"

Neville stared at me for a long time. He wanted me to follow his logic, but I had absolutely nothing.

"So her real name isn't Lucy Ferguson..." I said.

"Which means..." he said, patiently.

"That she has another name..." I said, waiting for him to finish my sentence. He didn't. "...and we don't know that name for sure."

"Continue," he said.

"And then... I guess...she may be using that name to..." I really wished he'd tell me something, but it seemed that he wanted me to find it out by myself. "I don't know the rest."

"You're doing great," he said.

I should probably have been looking for another job instead of partaking in those riddles. Maybe I should think back. Lucy had said her real name was Catherine Brown. Her dead father had a different name as well. What did that mean?

A man was reading a newspaper at the table next to ours. There was a picture of a car accident on the front page. A weird image came to my mind: the real Manny Randel and his young daughter dying in a car accident or in a fire.

"Do you think...?" I said carefully, "that Manny Randel might have died and that she..."

"Exactly!" he said. "You see full the picture now?"

I smiled awkwardly. No, I didn't. But then again, I didn't believe Neville was being completely sincere about his own investigation. It was like he couldn't put the puzzle together himself and was manipulating me to do it for him.

"So this ginger girl is unhappy with her father," he said "She wants him dead for some reason, and figures she can make it look like he was our second Watson, and now she can apply the jigsaw crockery routine to get away with the murder."

"I'm completely lost," I said. "This is overcomplicated. Why would someone do something like that?"

Once again he seemed disappointed with me. "Don't you think it's smart?"

"I think it's a mess," I said. "And isn't this too much assumption? Anyway, who even knows Randel played Watson? He was barely credited. Why not use any of the other Watsons?"

"She was planning to put it in the media yesterday," he said. "Including his name."

"I'm starting to get a headache," I said. "Anyway, we have zero facts to back this up..."

"I don't understand you," Neville said. "You were the one who came by with all these crazy theories, and now I'm telling you were right. Why are you so reluctant now?"

He wasn't wrong about that, but the truth was that I felt like a kid playing Clue and claiming that Coronel Mustard was the killer just because he had a funny name. Neville and I definitely weren't detectives, and we weren't doing any real detective work.

"But why? That's the thing I can't figure out." I changed the subject, impatient. "Why did she bring you into all this? Why come to you at the convention? If the goal was to get to you there, then why trigger the fire alarm?"

"Deception!" Neville exclaimed emphatically. "It's all about deception! This woman wants us to spread the so-called 'Watson murders' in the press. That's why we can't wait any longer; we have to go to the police right now!"

"We'll be laughed at," I said. "This makes no sense whatsoever."

Neville's face was pathetic. He had given so much thought to that clunky murder plot and the fact I wasn't impressed by it.

"Wait," I said. "We can't go to the police now. Let's just wait and see if we can find anything concrete about what you said."

74

"For what?" Neville demanded with fury. "I told you, every second is precious! Who knows if she's waiting for me at home with a shotgun? Who knows if she isn't waiting for you? Who knows if…?"

"I'm sorry, ma'am," said the waiter at the table next to ours. "You can't smoke in here."

"I'm sorry!" said Lucy, and then got up and went to the ladies'. Sir Neville had his back to her, so he couldn't see the hand gesture she made to me. I followed her with my eyes, my heart pumping so hard it could just burst right there.

"You feeling well, son?" Neville asked me. Lucy stood there, instead of getting into the bathroom. If I didn't get up, Neville would look back and see her. Lucy knew that, and was using it to make me obey her.

"I got to go to the toilet," I said. "Just a second."

I got up and disappeared behind the folding screen that concealed the toilets' doors — thank heavens he couldn't see me entering the ladies'! — and found Lucy, bent over the sink at the mirror.

"What's happening?" I asked.

"Jerry, I believe that you need to…" she started saying, but then another woman entered the bathroom. She stared at me awkwardly for a moment and I had to get out. "I can't follow you now," Lucy said as I left. "But can I come by at your flat tonight?"

"Yes, you can," I said.

75

When I got out there was a small group of people around Neville. Somebody had recognised him as *The Baker Street Sleuth* actor, and that lunch had become an autograph session. I wanted to go back to the toilets and talk to Lucy, see what made her feel that way. But I didn't. I stood by Neville's side waiting for that group to leave us alone. It took forever.

CHAPTER NINE

Calabash Cookies

"We should have met at my place from the start," Neville said as he pulled his keys from his pockets. "Why did you suggest we meet at that dreadful restaurant?"

We couldn't talk in the restaurant any longer, not with so many people asking for autographs, so we decided to finish our talk at his house. Actually, he was the one who had decided to meet in a public place, but I preferred not to tell him. All I did was suggest Juliano's off the top of my head.

I couldn't stop thinking about Lucy's words. She wanted to tell me something really important in that bathroom. Now I had to wait until that night to find out what she really wanted. Neville and I entered his house, the Sherlock Holmes museum. He went to the kitchen and asked me to sit down on the couch.

"Hope you're not too hungry," he said from the kitchen. "I baked some biscuits this morning — hope they're still good."

"That's great!" I said, picking up and opening the brief bag and taking the letters out. "I'll take a look at these in the meantime."

Wished there was more I could take from those things, but they seemed so ordinary and uninteresting! They just didn't seem to fit into our case. But, with a closer look, something caught my eye. In some, if maybe not all of them, the punctuation seemed a little too careful. There were commas, colons, semicolons, exclamations, all at the right moments. A little weird, I thought, for a deranged fan trying to intimidate his object of fixation...

"Never had the chance to ask if you like my place," he said.

"It's amazing! You must lead a very exciting life!" I said, putting the letters away.

Neville served me a cup of tea. "I guess you could call it that," he said. "It's nice to see I've been an important part of people's lives."

Only then I realised I hadn't got his autograph yet. How bizarre! Two days ago I would have killed for a picture signed by that man. But now I had something better, if you could call it that. I was his…partner? Friend? Associate? Whatever you'd call it, I was a part of the game now, much more than just a regular fan.

"So, Sir Bartholomew," I said, "what about that *Dracula* picture? When will you begin filming?"

He gave me a sad smile. "I'm afraid Terence Stamp got the role."

"Really?" I asked.

"It happens." He sounded melancholy. "Let's talk a little more about these letters. You really think they don't mean anything?"

Neville offered me some biscuits with the tea. They were all in the shape of calabash pipes. "There may be something to them," I said, picking up a biscuit. "But I don't know… If our theory were right, why would the killer be going after you? I mean, he is supposed to be killing the Watsons."

"I'm positively sure that your theory is right, Jerry," he said, putting some sugar in his tea. "You have a great eye for this sort of thing."

I blushed. "Thank you!"

"So what you're saying is that these are two completely unrelated incidents," Neville said.

The biscuits were well good, though a bit too small. I picked up another one and said: "It may be. I'll have to take these letters home and give them a better look. Anyway, I believe you should be on guard."

"I have a gun," he said. "And I know how to use it."

"That's good."

He lit a cigarette, inhaled the smoke and blew it out of the window. "Do you have a gun?"

"No," I said. "And even if I had one I wouldn't know how to shoot properly."

"Well, you need protection as well," he said. "You should think of getting a gun. Actually, it's a little odd that a detective doesn't own one."

"I'm a bagger," I said.

He looked at me with his eyes opened wide. "Does that mean you work for the mob?"

I couldn't avoid laughing. "I'm a special kind of detective," I said, and it wasn't a complete lie.

He smashed his cigarette in an ashtray. "I imagine there are many kinds." He picked up another cigarette, gave it some thought and then put it back into the pack. "Then again, I'm not a detective myself. I'm just an old actor who used to play one."

"And you did it greatly!" I said, trying to express all my admiration for his work, as well as change the subject. "I must have watched each and every episode of *The Baker Street Sleuth* a million times!"

"That's nice," he said with a sad voice. "You know, it's been really a long time since I shot the final episode. Do you know what I've done in the meantime? Three plays, five movies and a bunch of special appearances. I've even made the pilot for a new series. It was going to be a comedy about a grumpy old man who moves into his married son's house and turns everyone's life around." He seemed to chew every word. His hands were playing with the cigarette pack, almost crunching it. "I love doing comedy," he said. "I wish I could have done more of that."

He stared at the window for a long time, lost in his thoughts. Then he smiled and turned to me. "But you don't want to hear about that!" he said. "Want an autograph?"

"I can wait," I said with a weak voice. "I have to go; I need to return the car to my brother."

"What happened to your car?" he asked. "Or do you always share it with your brother?"

"Oh, we bought it together, so we share it," I said, and it was a lie. My only contributions to the car were the petrol and a few scratches.

"Well, Jerry, thanks for the ride and for the help. Too bad I don't have the energy you have. We would be solving this case twice as quickly."

"Don't worry, Sir Bartholomew," I said. "We'll catch this killer soon enough." I added mentally: 'If there really is a killer to be caught.'

He offered me another biscuit. "Listen," he said, "you've been able to deduct a lot of things until now…almost as if you knew this story."

He was righter than he realised. I knew that story. I had seen it a million times. After so many years of people telling me that real life wasn't like television, I saw myself in an investigation where things were pretty much like a TV episode. I felt like the future was predictable, almost certain.

"Tell me," he said, with a quirky smile. "How would things go from here on?"

I tried to think about it. If I was a *Baker Street Sleuth* writer, I believe it would be time to make things a bit more complicated. Maybe that series of murders wasn't simply being used to disguise a common crime. Maybe it was something bigger, something to deal with State affairs, something that could put the whole of England in danger. And that would be the time to introduce Mycroft Holmes, Sherlock's older and more intelligent brother, who didn't live up to his potential because he was too lazy. Somebody either in Her Majesty's secret service, or in some sort of private organization. I hadn't the slightest clue of how that would fit in the case; in fact, the whole thing was already complicated enough, but it would surely spice things up.

"So, what's on your mind?" he asked me, sounding genuinely interested.

I smiled at him and said: "I don't think this is how things should be done."

"What do you mean?" he asked me.

I picked up another biscuit and ate it slowly.

CHAPTER TEN

My Brother Pete

After dropping Neville at his place, I finally took the car back to Pete's, resigning myself to the inevitable lecture about how I wasn't doing anything with my life. I didn't think he'd think highly of my current endeavours. Despite that, it would be nice to talk to someone who still lived in the normal world. Also, I was really eager to grab a bite. I only had half a salad at the restaurant and a few biscuits at Neville's place. I doubted anyone would be buying me a hot meal in the near future.

Pete lived in a nice neighbourhood, even nicer than Neville's. My sister-in-law, Kara, was a kindergarten teacher; Pete worked from home as a financial consultant. My brother had always been the number one son, the pride of our parents. I was the disappointing son, the let-down. That wasn't to say that we didn't still get on; Pete and Mom and Dad and I all still kept in touch, though I had to say that relations weren't quite as good as they used to be. Life, you know; we'd all just gone our separate ways.

I parked in the driveway and knocked on Pete's door, hoping it was him, not his wife, who opened it. If I really had to listen to a sermon, I preferred to hear it from him. But, as you might have noticed, it wasn't my lucky day. The door opened and there was Kara with baby Norman in her arms. She wasn't pleased to see me. It was mutual.

"Hi, Jerry," she said. Her eyes flicked past me to the car. "Glad to see you've finally decided to return our car."

"Happy to see you too, Kara."

"I would be happier to see the milkman," she said sourly. "At least he's doing something useful with his life. "

Can't say I'd missed the reminders that my life was a failure. "Please, Kara," I said, hoping to move past the pleasantries and actually get in the house, "I…"

"Peter's in his office," Kara said, cutting me off. "He's very busy right now with work, but I guess I can knock at the door and see if he wants to see you."

"Okay," I said, following her into the house. "Any chance I can nab a sandwich?"

"A sandwich?" Kara stared at me.

"Yes," I said, embarrassed. "But not for now! I'll make two or three, if that's okay, and then take them away in a Tupperware for later…"

I trailed off. I'd never felt as low in my life as I did right then. There I was, Jerry Bellamy, worthless as a cockroach. Kara held Norman tighter to her chest, like she was afraid I would eat him. And I would have, if he were a sandwich.

"You…brought a Tupperware."

"Actually, I was thinking I could borrow one…"

Kara led me to the kitchen without saying another word, settled Norman in his high chair and went to knock on Pete's door. They had a nice big kitchen, with a gigantic fridge. I was jealous. The whole house was huge. They had lots of bathrooms, expensive furniture and a beautiful garden in the back that was almost ruined by a weird, triangle-shaped iron sculpture. I was glad that Kara was going to bring Pete to the kitchen, because I would get lost in there if I had to go after him by myself. I made four sandwiches and was about to grab a beer when Pete arrived.

"What did you get into this time?" he asked with a disapproving voice.

I was just closing the Tupperware when he appeared at the kitchen door, dressed in a pink linen shirt, brown pullover and corduroy pants. Quintessentially British. I was still wearing the same crumpled t-shirt I'd met Clive Louvagh in the previous day.

"Hi, Pete!" I said, biting into a piece of chocolate I'd found in the fridge. "I brought your car."

"Kara said." He looked me over. "She also said you looked like a bum. She was right."

I shut the fridge door, holding my Tupperware tight. He could say anything he wanted. He could bash me with words, humiliate me, put me on my knees and make me feel even lower than I already did. But I knew one thing for sure: when I got the bus back home, I'd have those sandwiches with me. I had my priorities in order.

"So, what's happening?" Pete asked. "Is it drugs?"

It had never been drugs, and Pete knew that. It was just a constant reminder that I was the failure. I'd never had problems with drugs, but to Pete — to Mom and Dad — I'd always been in trouble, and so it was only a matter of time before I got tangled up with drugs, too.

85

"I quit my job, Pete. I'm in a new line of work now." Well, that was a generous way of putting it. No need to mention that actually I'd been sacked and my new "job" didn't involve any recompense.

"Really?" Pete sounded sceptical. "And what is this new job?"

"I'm doing a lot of…research."

"Research?" Pete raised his eyebrows. "And what are you researching? The life of some actor from a TV show, I bet. That has always been your thing."

"Actually," I said, raising my voice, "that's exactly what I do in my new line of work."

"And I suppose you'll go around talking about movie trivia and borrowing my car for the rest of your life, huh? Jesus, Jerry, what are you doing with your…"

"Oh, I knew you would use those words," I said, getting mad. "Nothing I ever do with my life is going to be good enough for old Mr Ideal, with his ideal life, his ideal wife and his adorable ideal child?"

"You have no right to talk to me like that in my house!"

"I don't give a damn whose house this is," I said. "I'm doing something important, Pete! Something that matters! I don't care if you're proud of me; that's kid's stuff. Don't be my dad, just be my brother."

We stared at each other for a long time. We were always like that, the fighting Bellamy brothers. First we said everything we had to say. Then, we silently apologised and tried to start the whole conversation again.

"Want a beer?" said Pete.

"Thought you'd never ask."

We opened a couple of bottles and sat on the living room couch.

"So, tell me more about this new job of yours," he said. "What kind of research do you do?

"Do you mind if I eat while we talk?"

He shrugged.

"Okay," I said around a mouthful. "My client is an old TV star." I spoke and chewed at the same time. "He's been having some trouble with an old co-star and now he needs me to help him get rid of this guy."

"Sounds like detective work to me," Pete said.

"Yes," I said, though in reality the only license I had was a fake one. "That's precisely what I am: a private detective. But a very particular kind of detective. I'm a...TV detective."

"A what?"

"I invented it, which means I'm the only one in the world. You see, most people think that sitting in front of the TV all day is a useless activity. But think about it: the whole world passes through television. Everything you need to know, every bit of information, every detail is there."

"Is the money any good?" he asked, trying not to patronise me.

"One can make a living," I said.

That was a complete lie. Of course I wasn't going to tell him there was no money, for the same reason that I wasn't going to tell him that I wasn't a real detective. But I was comfortable with my new position. I wasn't doing anything great, but it was nice to be doing *something*.

"I worry about you, Jerry," he said. "Sometimes I worry a lot."

"You had no obligation to take care of me, Pete," I said.

He smiled and drank some beer. "You know, at this time of day I shouldn't."

A loud siren interrupted our talk. Pete's car alarm was going off outside. Pete jumped from the couch and ran to the front door; I followed. Somebody had thrown a rock through the windshield and there were pieces of glass everywhere. The rock was wrapped in a piece of paper, with a message on it: "Stop right where you are!"

"I can't believe it!" I said. "They found me!"

Pete turned to look at me. "What are you talking about?"

All I could do was repeat those three words: "They found me!"

Kara appeared at the front door, but Pete told her to go back inside and take care of Norman. "Did you bring this to me, Jerry?" Pete asked, and there was fear in his voice.

"I didn't..."

"Did you bring something dangerous to my family?" He sounded furious now.

"I…"

"I can't believe it!" He took a deep breath and then said, more calmly, "And for a moment I was starting to believe your story about being a 'TV detective'! This is…"

"Please listen, I…" I started, but then realise that talk wouldn't work. Pete ran back into his house. I didn't follow him. He'd be much better without me, in his perfect life. I just turned my back to his house and started walking back home. The beer bottle was still at my hand, but I had forgotten the Tupperware inside the house.

CHAPTER ELEVEN

Confessions

After being kicked off of the bus for trying to take a free ride, I had to walk back home. It was nearly dark as I got to my front door, and Lucy was sitting at the doorstep, waiting for me. I almost wished she wasn't. I had a lot on my mind and didn't want to deal with her at that moment.

"Hi, Jerry," she said. "You seem to be having a crazy day."

"That's a good way of summing it up," I said.

"You want me to come inside?" she asked.

"Sure."

We entered and sat on the couch, staring awkwardly at each other. The whole situation was odd. I felt like telling her everything that had happened since we split up at the restaurant. I also wanted to ask her what she had wanted to tell me in that bathroom before we got interrupted. But I didn't have the energy to have another talk like that. I was so tired of everything! All I wanted was to make love to her and sleep all night long, wake up and forget the whole thing.

Lucy apparently wanted the same. She took me by the hand and we walked together to the bedroom. What would Sherlock Holmes, with his brilliant, cold, emotionless mind, think of me, the TV detective, going to bed with one of my prime suspects? But I kept ignoring that. She was using me, but at least was giving me something nice in return. And even if she had second intentions —

and she most certainly did — I had never been given so much tenderness in my life. Maybe that's why I got so obsessed with her so fast.

I'd had sex with three girls before Lucy and none of them were that memorable. I was sixteen when I lost my virginity. My parents were out of town and Pete decided to throw a party at our house. I didn't want to stick around, but didn't have anywhere else to go. So I stayed in my room, reading comics, and then a girl entered the room. She was a couple of years older than me and was smoking a joint. She just jumped into my bed and started taking her clothes off. I was a bit scared, but took the opportunity. It didn't last long and I never saw her after that — to be honest, I never even asked her name. It took me four years to have sex again, this time with a hooker. I didn't like the experience and vowed never to pay for sex again. Then, when I was twenty-three, I met a girl named Caroline Young at a *Star Wars* convention and we dated for some time. She was the closest I'd ever had to a girlfriend. We stayed together for three weeks and had a lot of sex in this period. Then we simply stopped calling each other. I've seen Caroline at other conventions and each time she's accompanied by a different guy.

Lucy was completely different than all of them. At first I was afraid she'd be too mechanical, given the fact she had jumped in bed with me to keep me under a leash. But when we were naked in that bed she kissed me with such passion I forgot that idea. She couldn't be faking it all. She smelled so nice, her breasts were so soft and her tongue so delicious I completely surrendered to her. Almost an hour later we were lying on the bed, completely satisfied. And I had a proud smile on my face.

"Tell me more about you," I said, later that night. "Tell me something that doesn't concern the case."

"Like what?"

"What plays have you been in?" I said.

She settled her head against my shoulder. "Two years ago I was in a small production of *A Dog's Will*. I played the baker's wife. It was a good role, but there wasn't exactly a full house. Then I tried my hand at children's plays, and played the protagonist's brother's girlfriend in *A Touch of Magic*. It wasn't *Macbeth*, but it paid the rent. It also got me a larger role in another play…" She stopped and ran her fingers along my arm. "Are you really interested in hearing this?"

"Sure I am!"

"I was a fairy in *Cinderella*, at the Diamond." I could hear the smile in her voice. "After that I was Elektra in a Greek theatre festival, my biggest role to date. I wish Dad had lived to see that one. He loved the Greek classics."

"Sounds like a good role," I said.

"It was nice," she said. "For a moment I thought I'd start getting bigger roles, but things didn't work out. I started to get a few gigs as a continuity supervisor. I've been working in it for the last year. I've always had an eye for this kind of thing. Nobody can stand watching a movie with me; I'm always nit-picking every mistake."

I laughed. "Do you like it?"

"There are worse jobs," she said. "But it's not the kind of thing a little girls dreams of becoming. I guess I'm a part-time detective now."

She was getting close to talking about the investigation again, so I changed the subject.

"At least your career is interesting," I said. "I started as a griller in a deli, but got fired because my burgers were too greasy. Then I worked as a doorman in an old building, until they decided they didn't need a doorman at all. Meanwhile I tried to become a writer, but nobody would publish my stuff, so I abandoned that, too."

"I would love to read something you wrote!"

"Oh, trust me, you wouldn't. I tried hard, but it wasn't any good. They were just a bunch of detective stories and spy mumbo jumbo, but with no soul. I never managed to give my characters any distinct personality other than 'the tough guy', or 'the damsel in distress'."

"I would like to read it anyway."

"And why is that?" I asked.

"I don't know. You are an interesting guy. Ever since we met, you've put all your energy into everything you do. I bet you can write great stories."

I couldn't remember the last time someone had complimented me like that. It might have been in Year 6, when I made a really great drawing of the Prime Minister. I couldn't remember now who had been Prime Minister at the time. Lucy was telling me I was an interesting guy, and she was in my bed, completely naked, so my mind was otherwise occupied. This was much better than a drawing of the Prime Minister.

"And when did you become a detective?" she asked. Had I ever told her I was a detective? Couldn't remember. Anyway, my Lestrade ID was in my trouser pocket by the bed, just in case.

"Well, it was after I quit my last job."

"What did you do?"

"I was a bagger at a quick market. A really shitty one, for that matter."

She looked at me with surprise, blinking those big blue eyes.

"Really?"

"Yeah."

I expected her to go away that very moment, but she just stared at me and smiled. "You must be the most interesting person I've ever met," she said.

"Really?" I asked, genuinely surprised.

"Yes," Lucy said. "I'm glad we've met. Only wish it'd been in a different scenario. I mean, I don't think you'd introduce me to your mother, given the way we met."

"Would you introduce me to your dad?"

Her smile got a bit sadder. "I think he'd like you. Dad was a man of heart. I don't ever remember him being angry with someone who didn't deserve it. He had two passions in the world: me and acting.

94

Losing his career was the worst thing that could have happened to him. He would probably have jumped off a bridge if he hadn't had me. So I became his pupil, and he did his best to make me an actress."

"He did a great job."

Her smile got even sadder and a couple of tears ran down her face.

"*The Baker Street Sleuth* was just a short gig to him," she said. "They wanted him to become Duvall's official body double. It wasn't what he really wanted, but the money was okay." Lucy wiped her face with her bare arm. "But he and Neville had a big argument during the shooting, and he decided to leave. Little did he know it would be the end of his career."

I remained silent, and thankfully Lucy didn't say another word, either. Soon we slept together in each other's arms, and would have stayed like that until the sun rose. Unfortunately, somebody had other plans for that night.

CHAPTER TWELVE

Conspiracy Peanuts

It was one in the morning when they started ringing the doorbell. It didn't wake Lucy up, and that at least was a relief. I opened my eyes in the dark and it took me some time to realise that the bell wasn't part of my dreams. It was annoying as hell, and it kept going. I really wished I could ignore it until whoever it was gave up and left us alone. But whoever it was wouldn't stop ringing, so I got up, trying not to make any noise, and put on some trousers and a shirt. I went to the living room and opened the door slowly. Neville didn't know where I lived, and the chances Pete would ring my bell at one in the morning to make friends again were slim. I couldn't think of anyone else, but so many things had already happened I told myself nothing could surprise me anymore.

"Mr Bellamy?" said the man outside my flat. He was wearing a black suit and dark glasses and had greasy hair. He had a Martin Scorsese smile on his face, the kind of smile that doesn't invite you to share the joke.

"Wrong flat, mate," I said, and tried to close the door in his face. Scorsese held the door with his foot.

"I'm positively sure you're the one I'm looking for," he said. "Put on some shoes. I'll wait."

"Okay," I said, "but my shoes are in the bedroom."

He nodded.

I went to the bedroom and scribbled a hasty note for Lucy. There wasn't time to write anything detailed, so all I scrawled was that I'd be back soon and that she shouldn't worry. Those might be my final words, but just then I had no problem that they were all lies.

I was escorted downstairs to a big black sedan.

"In," said my escort.

I held my breath and entered the car.

My escort joined me, making three of us in the back, with one in front to drive. The man sitting across from me was dressed similarly to the man who had first come to the door; there wasn't a hint of a smile on his face as he, somewhat incongruously, worked his way through a bag of peanuts. Scorsese kept silent during the ride.

"Sorry to disturb you this time of night, Bellamy," he said pleasantly. "We've been watching you for the last couple of days."

"I didn't notice," I said.

"I didn't think so. We're very good at being invisible. Right now I have transcriptions of every single word you said since you got out of that TV convention."

"You mean you had people wired?" I asked.

"What do you think?" he said, grabbing some more peanuts.

"I think that is quite impossible."

He didn't like that. "So, a smart guy," he said. "You better watch your mouth."

"I should have done that days ago," I said. "Right now I'm not sure it'd make a difference."

"Let's talk business," he said.

"Who are you?" I asked. "And what kind of business are we supposed to talk about?"

The car was moving, and soon we were out of my neighbourhood. The streets were mostly empty, except for a few occasional vehicles that passed by our windows. It was all pitch dark and very silent. They could do whatever they wanted with me, but somehow I wasn't afraid.

"Listen, Bellamy," said the peanut man, without looking directly at me. "I'm pretty sure that by now you've realised there is more to this case than some pretty girl and an actor past his prime."

I nodded, even though I hadn't really figured that out completely. But, come to think of it, things were never so simple in TV, so why should they be so in real life?

"So, what do you want to talk about?" I asked. "I'm pretty sure that you have a team of super-qualified agents working around the clock to keep you informed, so why the hell would you need the help of a TV detective?"

"A what?" he asked me.

"A TV detective. It's just something I...oh, never mind. What do you want with me?"

He ate some more peanuts, seeming a little confused. "As I told you, we're here to talk business. You have gotten yourself in a pretty messy situation."

"I guess you could call it that," I said. "Am I in the middle of some international intrigue? Are you going to hire me to stop the Cold War from coming back?"

"You're too dramatic," said the peanut man.

I shrugged. "Things haven't been very simple these last couple of days."

"So just sit and listen," he said.

"I'm already sitting," I replied. "But I imagine that is the easy part."

"They told me you were funny." He didn't sound amused. "Here's the sitch: I work for some very wealthy people. I can't really tell you any names, but let's just say they are directly interested in what you're doing."

"Can't you be more specific?" I said. "I could use a little more information, if you really want me to help you."

"You've just used the magic word," he said. "It's all about information. The most precious commodity these days. As I've told you, I work for some really powerful people, people who control most of this country's information systems. But there's always something that escapes our eyes."

"Am I one of these things that escaped your eyes?" I asked.

"Don't flatter yourself," the peanut man said, sounding a little angry. "You are just a pawn in this game."

99

"Enlighten me, then," I said. "Who are these people we're dealing with? Mobsters? Spies? Aliens? I don't know about Neville, but I took a very good look at the girl and didn't see any tentacles."

"Do me a favour, would you?" He was beginning to lose his temper, probably because the movie trailer talk wasn't having the effect he planned on me. "We need your help. I'm not going to lie to you, Bellamy; we have at least a dozen men that could work this out better than you can. But they are not involved in this, not like you are. You're very well positioned inside this whole charade."

The guy was so vague it was impossible for me to give him a serious answer. Once again, I was confronted with a character straight out of a TV show. That was a funny thought. I should probably get mad at how absurd the whole thing had gotten, but then I realised that I could play a character, too. I could be the TV detective, and instead of being just a watcher of the game, I could be one of the players. Hell, I could even win it!

"If you want my help in this case," I said in a serious voice, "you have to tell me something more." I gave it some thought and then added, "Unless you are only here to waste my time, in which case I'm afraid we'll have to say goodbye."

He smiled at me. It was the kind of smile that said 'welcome to the play'. I had to get a grip on myself in order not to smile back. "Tell me something, Bellamy," he said. "How well do you know Bartholomew Neville? And how well do you know that girl you're sleeping with?" Once again I shrugged. "It seems to me that you have an awful habit of trusting people you don't know."

The driver took a turn back and was returning to my neighbourhood. They'd taken me for a short ride. "I don't know you," I said. "But I'm listening to what you're saying. Not because I believe you, but because this is what I have to do."

"So I guess you know where I'm going with this," the peanut man said.

"Not really, but it is taking some very interesting turns," I answered.

"I'm glad you're amused," he said sarcastically.

"And what is the mission, after all?" I asked him. "Should I keep my ears open? Pay attention to details? Trust nobody? Did I forget any clichés? Why don't you tell what you really want?"

He sighed. "Listen, here's what you have to know. Lucy Ferguson is in possession of some top-secret information, but still isn't able to use it. And you are helping her to figure out how to use it."

"You mean Lucy's a blackmailer?" I tried to take that seriously, but it wasn't easy. "And how am I helping her?"

He opened another pack of peanuts. "Think about it. You have something that can pull a country apart. But it's like having a lot of bullets with no gun."

"So, I'm the gun?" I asked.

"No. She's using you to find the gun."

"Could you be more specific?" I asked, a little pissed off. "Who is she blackmailing? Who should I be protecting?"

"I've already told you everything I can," he said.

"Won't you even tell me what I'm supposed to do?"

The car stopped, and we were suddenly in front of my building again. "Keep your ears open," he said. "Pay attention to details. Trust nobody. Oh, and wait for our next contact."

"Really?" I asked. "You took me out of bed for this? Don't I get to know anything else?"

The driver opened the door for me to get out.

"It's good enough for now," said the peanut man. "We'll be in touch again."

Before getting out of the car, I asked him one last question: "Was this whole thing really necessary?"

"Why wouldn't it be?" he asked me back.

Scorsese was about to shut the door, but I held it open. "So I guess I'll be seeing you soon," I said. "But I'm not sure you are getting everything you want from me."

"That would be too bad for both of us," the peanut man said.

"Just one more thing. Do you have a name?" I asked. "It doesn't have to be the name your mother gave you, but I'd like to have something to call you by."

He crushed the empty peanut pack and threw it by the open door into the gutter. "What name would you prefer?"

"Can I call you Mycroft?" I said.

He frowned very hard. In fact, suspiciously hard. "What kind of name is that?"

I shrugged "I thought you might know it."

"Call me Bill. It's a lot simpler," he said and shut the door. Soon the car turned around the corner. I waited for a while and came back to the flat.

CHAPTER THIRTEEN

So Long

Lucy woke up before me again, but this time she didn't prepare breakfast. Instead, she gave me a wake up nudge and practically shoved the piece of paper I'd left for her in the night in my face.

"'I'll be back soon. Don't worry.' What the hell is this?"

How could I be so stupid? After the Bill episode I'd just come back to bed and forgotten the note. Who was the brilliant guy now?

"Oh, that… I couldn't sleep and went out for a walk, but I didn't want you to wake up and be worried if I was still out."

"You went for a walk?" she said. "In the middle of the night?"

Lucy got up and got dressed. She was furious. I didn't know what to say to her. It didn't seem like a good idea to tell her what had really happened. Partly because it would make her even angrier, but also because it was so absurd she wouldn't believe it. I wasn't sure if I believed it myself.

"Are you going away?" I asked. "Because I don't know what's going to happen if you do."

"I'll tell you what will happen," she said while putting his shoes. "We are going to be against each other. You're going to help my father's killer to build his case and frame somebody else."

"Don't be so dramatic over a note," I said.

"Don't tell me what to do," Lucy said, with tears in her eyes. "God, I feel so cheap! Actually, less than that. Going to bed with a stranger to gain his confidence and ending up betrayed like this. What would my dad say?"

Lucy was on her way to the door when I grabbed her by the arm. I don't know why I did that. The best thing would be letting that crazy chick go away and take care of my own business. She said I was a cold-hearted bastard, so maybe I should be one. But I couldn't. I had grown too fond of Lucy to let her think so many bad things of me.

"Listen to me," I said, trying not to be too patronising. "I haven't picked sides yet. This is all crazy. I mean, I had this crazy idea about a series of murders, and that idea just turned out to be real. I wasn't expecting any of this when I went to Neville's place to tell him my theories. It was just some crazy fanboy shit, but it turned out to be real. But now the whole world seems to be this weird fan fiction, and anything can happen."

"What do you mean?" she asked me, tears in her eyes. I told her everything that happened while she slept. Lucy stared at me with an astonished look on her face. "This is crazy," she said. "You can't believe in all that."

"I'm not sure if I do," I said. It was really quite confusing. But at the same time, it was really exciting. I didn't want to tell Lucy, but I was enjoying it quite a bit. After years watching other people's adventures on the TV screen, I finally had my own mystery to investigate, and it was full of dark secrets, conspiracy theories and mysterious strangers with dramatic speeches. I didn't want to go back to my normal, boring life. I liked the way things were turning out to be. But of course I wasn't going tell her all that. It wasn't a

105

game to Lucy. She had lost her father to the killer we were going after. It was about justice to her. "I haven't figured out whose side I'm on," I finally said.

"You have to choose," she said. "I don't like the idea that you think I'm behind all this."

She wiped her tears with her fingers, trying not to look me in the eye. "Back there, in the restaurant toilets," I said. "You wanted to tell me something, didn't you?"

She nodded. "It was a silly thing."

"What was it?" I asked.

Lucy stared at me with angry eyes. I didn't know if it was real anger or just an excuse to avoid the subject. "I don't want to tell you anything. Will you let me go?"

"Lucy, please…" I tried to calm her down, but she reached for her purse and took the panic button out of it.

"You want me to press this button?" she asked. "Then you can have a nice chat with the police." She was crying now. "Maybe I should do it. Maybe I should have done this from the start. Let them handle this business. Things would be much easier now. Too bad I had to fall for the romantic idea of avenging my dad with my own hands."

She was soaked in tears and couldn't speak any more. I grabbed her in my arms and let her cry.

"What is going on with you, Lucy? It isn't just Neville, is it?" I asked her.

She tried to calm down. "No," she said, "and yes. Sorry to put you into all this. Why did you have to be there? Things would be so different if you hadn't got involved in all this."

She stepped back, drying her tears with her hands. "You don't have to tell me anything," I said. "You owe me nothing, Lucy. But right now I got to go. There's something important going on, and I'm right in the middle of it." I stopped for a moment, trying to figure out how to tell her what I felt. "For the first time in my life I'm involved in something big. I can't let this go."

I expected Lucy to be mad at me, slap me and call me a selfish prick. To my surprise, she just looked tired. "Do what you have to do, then," she said. "Be a detective. Just don't expect me to be the femme fatale in this story."

She walked past me and went to the door.

"Will I ever see you again?" I asked.

"I'd like to," she said. "But only when this is all over."

"'When this is all over'?" I repeated, confused. "Are you going to give up?" Lucy didn't want to make eye contact with me. She seemed ashamed. Her lips were trembling, not because she was about to cry or anything, but because she wanted to say something. But she didn't. "Weren't you pursuing revenge a second ago?"

"Fuck you," she said, turning her back and going away. I should have followed her, but I didn't. Lucy was an enigma and I didn't think I could solve her at the moment. I went back to my bedroom and lay down on the bed, fake ID in hand.

The phone ring woke me up just before dawn. It was Neville. "We have a funeral to attend," he said. "Be here at eight o'clock."

"Who died?" I asked.

"Watson," he said, and added dramatically: "Again."

PART TWO — MOSAIC

CHAPTER ONE

The Woman in the Plaster

"So glad you're here, lad!" Neville said as I walked into the house. He closed the door and followed me, saying: "So much to be done! We'll make a quick stop to get you a suit. We still have a little time before the reception."

He was very presentable, wearing a grey suit and a fedora, ready to give a great performance. I looked like shit, but then again, I was only his sidekick. All I had to do was make him look good. In comparison with me, anyone would.

"I thought you said we were going to a funeral," I said.

"A funeral reception," he said. "It's not easy to talk to the dead man's family in church."

We took a cab and stopped by a tailor shop where Neville had credit. In less than half hour we were back on the road, and I had a fairly nice suit on.

"You look better," Neville pronounced as we got in the cab. "Now, we need to do a little rehearsal."

"Rehearsal?" I asked, confused.

"We don't want people to know we are investigating this series of murders yet," he said.

"Why not?" I asked. "Sooner or later people will know. If anything, the other Watsons will be safer knowing they're in danger."

"Trust me, okay? I've done this a million times."

"On TV, you mean," I said, but was too tired to insist.

"Just listen, would you? I have a plan. I'll be playing the role of Bartholomew Neville, an old colleague actor of the late Lewis Thompson, who's there to pay a final tribute to his former co-star."

I frowned "Isn't that exactly who you are?"

"Yes, except for the fact I didn't even remember the man's existence before you came to me the other night," he said. "You'll be playing Jerry Bellamy, my biographer, who needs to know positively everything he can about the deceased man in order to write about him."

"That seems unnecessarily complicated," I said. "Why can't I just continue pretending I'm a detective?"

"Aren't you a detective?" he asked, surprised.

"Yours is a great plan," I said, trying to change subjects. Being flattered was clearly Neville's weak spot. He immediately forgot what he was talking about. The truth was his plan wasn't that great. It actually was quite stupid. A biographer asking questions at a funeral wouldn't be much different than a nosy journalist. People would get either annoyed or offended by my curiosity, and that would make things harder instead of easier. A detective, on the other hand, would have the reasons and the authority to do so. But Neville was having fun creating an elaborate hoax, and I decided to play along.

"Very well," he said as we stopped in front of the restaurant where the reception was taking place. "Shall we go, then?"

"Just a second, Sir Bartholomew... I..."

And then I started to cry. Just out of nowhere. My face was red and I was crying like a baby. I didn't want to do that in front of my biggest idol, and especially not now that we were working together, but I just exploded. It wasn't supposed to be like this. If anyone had ever told me I'd be in this cab, with this man, trying to find a killer, I would find it too awesome to be real. But now that I was here, all I wanted was to go away and go back to my normal, shitty life. I didn't want to be his sidekick. In a way, it was a dream come true. In many others, it was an awful nightmare.

Neville didn't try to comfort me or anything, just stared at me with a pretty bland look, waiting for me to calm down. I took a deep breath. The best thing to do was to get in character again.

"Sorry about that," I said.

"Are you okay?" he asked.

"I don't know if I should go," I said, feeling miserable.

"It's a funeral reception, my dear lad. Nobody will find it odd if you start crying."

The last time I'd been to one of those was at seventeen, when my grandmother died. Those receptions were always very sad and I didn't feel comfortable crashing one. I tried to keep in mind that the whole thing was about saving the lives of the other Watsons, and that thought made me feel a bit better.

"I'll talk to Mrs Thompson," Neville said as we entered. "Blend into the crowd and see what you can find."

I looked around, trying to figure out where to start. The first person to catch my eye was a middle-aged woman in a blue dress with pale blonde hair and tiny eyes. She was the only mourner not wearing black, but she was also the only one with an arm in a cast and a black eye. I went up to her and said hi.

"Hello," she answered, without looking at me.

"Are you a relative?" I asked. "Of the dead guy, I mean."

She gave me a funny look, and I realised I probably shouldn't have said 'dead guy' like that.

"My name is Amanda," she said. "The dead guy was my uncle." She studied me for a moment and then added, "I was the one who found him."

"How did that happen?"

She stared at me in disbelief. Thinking about it, I figured it might be wiser to apologise and get the hell out of there. But then the anger melted away and she gave a tired sigh.

"I'm sorry for the questions," I said, and offered my hand. "My name is Jerry Bellamy. I'm Sir Bartholomew Neville's biographer." I pointed him out.

"Sherlock Holmes?" she asked, ignoring my hand and glancing quickly at him. "Imagine that! Uncle Lewis said Neville couldn't care less about his co-stars!" She shook her head. "I guess he was wrong."

"Neville is devastated," I said. "Your uncle was his favourite co-star. I'd hoped to interview him, for the book, you know, but then... I'm sorry for your loss."

"Thank you," she said. "We all loved Uncle Lewis very much."

"He seemed to be a very...generous man."

"I wouldn't say generous." There was bitterness in her voice. "At least, not after hearing his will. And to think he always told me I was his favourite niece."

"Do you think I could put that in the book?" I said, jokingly.

"I'd prefer you didn't," she said. "Though there are a few things to be said about the whole situation."

"Like what?"

She almost smiled at me, but then went back to her grieving face. "Tell me, Mr. Bellamy," she said, with excitement in her voice, "what kind of biography are you writing? Are you interested only in patronising your client, or are you getting dirty?"

I spotted a chance there. "I'm not supposed to tell you this," I said, "but my editor wants something explosive. Would you like to make a contribution?"

She looked around, like she was afraid somebody would listen to her.

"I don't want you to think I like gossip," she said. "But there are a few weird things in Uncle Lewis's death."

"How come?" I asked.

"Aunt Claire was away for the afternoon," she said, "and she asked me to pay a visit to Uncle Lewis. I rang the bell a few times and since he didn't answer, I took the spare key from under the rug and looked for him all over the house. When I opened the cellar door and looked down at the bottom of the stairs, I saw Uncle Lewis lying in a strange position. I ran downstairs to see if he was okay, but one of the steps was broken, and I felt downstairs over his...well, over his corpse."

"Really?" I said. "What was he was doing downstairs?"

"He had a small office in the cellar. He was working on his memoirs. He was very fond of his days in the theatre, and started this silly book about two months ago. He practically lived in the cellar."

"You said you fell down the stairs?"

"It was an old wood brick staircase, and one of the bricks had fallen off, probably under my uncle's feet. It was a very unexpected death."

"And his memoir... Do you think you can get me a copy? It would be a great contribution to my book."

"I don't think so," she said. "The other members of the family might not like it."

"Oh, that's too bad..." I said, sounding overly disappointed. "Well, I guess I'll give this whole thing a paragraph or too."

She looked as disappointed as I expected her to. "I'm really sorry."

"I understand," I said. "My editor would really love to take a look at it."

"Your editor?" she asked me, and the excitement was back.

"Yes. TV celebrities' memoirs are really a thing nowadays," I said, and added, "The publishing industry makes bestsellers out of unfinished books."

"Are you serious?" Amanda asked me. "The truth is, none of us has actually read it… in fact, very few people knew he was serious about this book. Most of the family thought it was just something to pass the time, but he was very dedicated to it." She came closer and whispered the next sentence. "I think he was writing something dangerous."

I whispered back: "Is the book in the will that you mentioned?"

"No."

"So I don't think any of the other relatives will claim the rights over it, will they?"

I had her right there. "I think I can get you a copy," she said, "if you can find a way to use it. Give me your address and I'll mail it to you in the next few days."

I gave her Neville's address and moved on. As I talked to other people at the funeral, I began to develop a clear picture of Lewis Thompson. The general consensus was that he'd been a nice man, beloved by many, and with a great passion for acting. He had a fine theatre career after *The Baker Street Sleuth*, and a few minor roles in movies. He had had fond memories of playing Watson, though he had only appeared in five episodes. Few people seemed aware that he'd been working on his memoirs, and the ones who knew it didn't seem to care much about it.

I was filling my pockets with canapés when I saw that a lot of people were gathering around Neville. They had all recognised him as the famous TV actor, which to him was a cue to start making a speech.

"This is a hard time for everyone, and I have no illusions that a few words will ease the grief we all feel right now." He paused, for dramatic effect I supposed, and then continued, "As you may know, Lewis and I co-starred on *The Baker Street Sleuth* in the 1988 series. But our bond went beyond that of co-stars. In those few months we worked together, it became clear to me that he was one of a kind. And though I unfortunately had not seen my old friend for many years — life contrives to separate even the best of friends — I never forgot his joy, his benevolence or the way he was able to bring a smile to my face even in my darkest moments. So I ask for all of you to have a moment of silence, for this man shall be greatly missed."

Everyone lowered their heads, except for me. I was observing Neville, who was again playing a role. This time I didn't know which one it was. I knew that he'd just said a bunch of lies, and I knew why he had told them. He hadn't seen Thompson in all those years, but when he made that speech, even the dead man would've believed him. I was starting to form a different image of Bartholomew Neville, one that looked more like a pompous prick than a man who had those kind of feelings towards a person he hadn't seen for almost a decade. It took me a few seconds after he was finished for me to realise he didn't care at all for the dead man or his family. I felt unclean and a little disturbed. If he was able to fool me when I knew he was lying, imagine what he could do when I didn't...

Prayer finished, Neville apologised to Mrs Thompson, explaining that he had to get back to the studio immediately to finish filming a movie, adding that he'd only been able to get a short break to attend the funeral.

It was unusually sunny outside. Neville kept that same pompous expression as we walked out, but I wasn't that cool-headed. I actually felt dirty and didn't want to be around him. But we had a case to solve, and I didn't forget that.

"Let's go back to my place," he said, looking for a cab. "We have lots to discuss."

"Don't you want to go to the pub?" I suggested. "I could really use a pint."

"At this time of day?" he asked.

I just shrugged. The truth was that I didn't want to be alone with him in his house. He was starting to give me the creeps.

CHAPTER TWO

How I Became a Detective

Thankfully, nobody recognised Neville while we were at the pub. The last thing I wanted was people coming by asking for autographs. We chose a discreet table and ordered some food and a couple of pints. I took off my jacket and loosened my necktie. Never saw the point of those things, anyway.

I drank half of my pint as soon as the barman brought it. My throat felt like the Sahara desert, mostly due to anxiety, and I still felt unclean. I had done some weird stuff in the previous couple of days, and some of them were probably illegal, but pretending to be something I wasn't to extract information from a grieving family had surely taken the cake. It didn't seem to affect Neville the least bit, though. He was staring at me with that creepy smile.

"I told you it was a good plan," he said.

I tried to smile back. Not sure if I succeeded. "I guess we got a good lead."

"This memoir will answer a lot of questions," he said, picking his pint of beer for the first time. "This is getting really exciting!" He really was enjoying this just a bit too much.

"It won't answer all of them," I said, trying to get a grip on him. "It won't tell us if Thompson was murdered."

"There is no doubt about that," he said. "Mrs Thompson told me she was at her sister's for the afternoon. Somebody could have damaged that step while the old fart slept. The killer could have just smothered the poor bastard with a pillow or stabbed him to death, but that wouldn't do. She wanted it to look as much like an accident as possible."

He seemed to be too certain about it, but I wasn't convinced yet. Sure, there was a part of me that believed Thompson's death was connected to the crimes we were investigating. Otherwise it would mean we were on the wrong track and that our whole investigation was a waste of time. But it just didn't fit our killer's modus operandi. Hadn't he killed the previous two Watsons with shots to the back? Why would he...

Only then I realised that that wasn't the pronoun Neville had used. "*She* wanted it to look like an accident?" I looked up from my food. "Do you still suspect Lucy?"

"I never had any doubt. But I still need to prove it to you."

"Yeah, right." I didn't believe it for a minute. It wasn't easy to pick sides. I didn't know much about Lucy and the little I knew could be a lie. On the other hand, Neville was becoming quite suspicious himself. He was always coming up with these crazy plans, over-complicated schemes and confusing theories that didn't seem to fit the case. Maybe the answer was much simpler than that.

"What else did you get from the widow?" I asked, reaching for the ketchup. "She must've read the memoir."

"Surprisingly, she hadn't," Neville said. "Her husband spent a lot of time in the cellar, writing, but she doesn't seem to believe there's anything important in those pages."

That was good. It meant Amanda wouldn't have much trouble taking the manuscript away from the house. I didn't think the memoir would close the case, but it sure was a good lead. After a couple of weeks I'd call Amanda, saying my editor wasn't interested. I only hoped the killer had already been caught by then.

"So, what do we do now?" I asked.

"We need to be patient," he said. "I don't think we should make any moves before we get our hands on that manuscript."

I rolled my eyes. He could afford to sit and wait. I couldn't even afford to pay for my burger, not to mention my phone, water and electricity bills. Usually I'd go to Pete and ask him to lend me some money, but that wasn't an option anymore. My financial situation had never been so desperate, and I should be looking for a job instead of playing detective.

Neville ate a chip and said, "Meanwhile, we need to find our next Watson: Jake Scott."

"And how would we do that?" I asked. "I don't think you kept in touch with him, did you?"

"You say that like it's a crime," he said. "We shot one episode together, and he was drunk all the time. Why do you think we reshot everything with another actor?"

He was right about that. Scott was supposed to be a replacement for Lewis Thompson, but was fired after one single episode, which was only aired once. I had a bootlegged copy of that episode, and he wasn't awful in it, but definitely bad. He was soon replaced by David Elroy, who stayed in the role to the end of the last series.

"Was he fired simply for being drunk?" I asked.

"Something to do with that," he said. "We brought him to the show due to his experience in soap operas. They said he was very professional, but he was something of prima donna and liked to act like he was the main star. On the last day of shooting, he jumped into the waterfall we were filming at and didn't die, by some miracle. We decided to cut him off before he created any more problems."

Could that be a lie? All those rumours about Neville being hard to work with came back to my mind. They said he could make the lives of his co-stars a living hell — and that didn't sound so hard to believe at that moment, especially after the scene at the reception. It was a little weird hearing him call someone else a prima donna. Lucy had said he sabotaged her father's career. I wondered what he might have done to Scott. I drank some of my beer and asked: "So, how are we going to find him?"

"I was a little concerned about that," he said. "But thankfully I have a great detective working for me."

"And who would that be?"

"You, of course!" His face lit up. "You're the one who figured out this whole conspiracy, and all you had was an actress with a funny voice and two words! I'm guessing it will be a piece of cake for you to find Scott."

That caught me completely by surprise. Maybe because I didn't expect that kind of praise to come out of his mouth. It was weird, especially considering how self-centred he had been until that moment. But then again, he could be saying that just to convince me to be on his side. On second thought, I might be being too harsh on him. Sure, he could be using me the same way he had used his fictional friendship with the late Lewis Thompson to gain the empathy of those people. But there was also a small chance he was being sincere. But that wasn't the problem. What really bothered me was the fact that I wasn't such a great detective. Damn, I wasn't a detective at all! I was still walking around with a fake badge, and sooner or later somebody would want to take a closer look at it. Plus, I had used some really weird methods to find out about the Watson killer, and even though they'd worked the first time, it wouldn't be so easy to use them to find a missing man.

"Sir Bartholomew, I don't…" I started, ready to decline the offer. I still wanted to be a part of the investigation, but couldn't accept that task. He'd have to hire a real detective.

"Is it a question of money? Don't worry," he said, waving a hand negligently. "I'll pay you the same amount you charge for any of your clients, no more, no less."

I gave that some thought. It was a tempting offer and I really needed the money. He still thought I was a detective and I somehow didn't feel dirty by fooling him. If he'd made that offer before the funeral reception, I'd probably have said no. But now I felt that if I wasn't around to watch Neville, he might do something dangerous. It was a weird thought, but I felt he shouldn't be on the case by himself, for his own security and for the security of everyone involved. And since I had no other plans for the immediate future, to say nothing of the rest of my life, this gig could really mean something. It would keep me busy, keep me afloat financially and, most of all, it might give a little meaning to my life.

"I'll find him for you," I said at last. "But I'll need you to pay me a week in advance. I have some bills to pay."

"That will be no problem," he said. "But we need to find him before she does."

'She'. That word again. It reminded me that I was being paid to be against Lucy. The problem was that I still hadn't picked a side, and wasn't ready to do it now.

I tried to concentrate on other aspects of the problem that didn't involve picking sides. There were two other men out there whose lives were in danger. I didn't know who wanted them dead, but if I could find Scott before the killer, maybe I could put an end to the carnage. That was good enough for the moment.

Neville and I finished our pints and he gave me some money. I had a job to do now. It was better to do it right.

CHAPTER THREE

On the Case

My flat still smelled like Lucy's perfume. I tried to ignore it, but if I closed my eyes I could imagine that she was there, and that if I went into the kitchen she'd be making dinner, witty retorts just waiting to fly into action in response to anything I said. Too bad this was reality. My flat was cold and empty, and if I was honest with myself, I doubted that Lucy would ever speak to me again.

It was odd standing in the flat, because everything else was in the same place. But now I was the proud owner of a very elegant suit and some advance money from Neville to take care of my detective costs in my pocket. It was enough to eat — no fancy dinners, but who's complaining?

I sat down on the floor and opened the briefcase Neville had given me, spreading the information about Jake Scott out in front of me. Besides Lucy's father, who'd only been a stand-in, Scott had been the briefest of all Watsons, and since his one episode was later reshot, only a few people remembered him.

Scott had appeared in "The Final Problem", one of the most vital episodes in the series, in which Sherlock Holmes faces his greatest enemy, Professor James Moriarty. Holmes and Moriarty have their final face-off at the Reichenbach Falls, after which Holmes is finally considered dead, only to come back in the next series. Of all the episodes *The Baker Street Sleuth* had produced, this had been the one that demanded the most of Watson, dramatically speaking. From what I remembered, Scott had acted a little too intensely. He hadn't done anything awful, but his reaction to Holmes's apparent death had been larger than life, as though he was trying to win a BAFTA on his first appearance. Then again, Neville tended to go a little over the top himself, and I'd never complained about that. But there was that other story, about him jumping from the waterfall. I could see them cancelling his contract over that.

But I still didn't believe that story. I could hear Lucy's voice in my head. "Neville is a viper," she'd said. She would have told me that Neville could have gotten Thompson fired simply because he was getting too good, or even because he wasn't licking Neville's boots. It was a possibility, and I didn't want to put it aside just because Neville was the one hiring me.

Neville hadn't given me much; it was mostly photos from the filming in Inversnaid, Scotland. I had to laugh at the irony; if I'd had these pictures a week earlier, I'd have been the happiest fanboy in England. The first photograph showed Neville fully dressed in Sherlock Holmes's cape and deerstalker hat; in the second, Jay Mortigan rehearsed his lines, half in costume as Moriarty. There were two photos of Jake Scott as Watson. In the first he was smoking a cigarette and playing chess with an unidentified man. The man was drinking from a shining green hip flask that had apparently been handed to him by Scott. They were both laughing and looked relaxed. In the second picture, Scott was sitting in an empty dining room with a nice fireplace, finishing a meal.

I stared at the last two pictures for half an hour, trying to find something crucial in either of them, but kept coming up empty. There was something strange there, but I couldn't figure out what it was. I had a feeling that there might be a piece of the puzzle missing, one that I'd only be able to identify once I'd gathered more information. So I turned my attention to the other materials that Neville had given me. Scott's resignation letter was in the case as well, crumpled and with a stain of mud on the corner, which probably meant the news hadn't been taken very well. It also meant that somebody (Neville?) had picked up the letter and kept it. But why? The contents of the letter weren't very friendly. The producer had apparently been outraged at Scott's behaviour during shooting in Scotland and had accused him of being an alcoholic.

There wasn't anything else in the briefcase, which meant that all I had were pieces. Pieces of a story and it was my job to put them together. There was something in there, for sure, something hiding, perhaps something Neville didn't want me to see. If Jake Scott had been an alcoholic, it was entirely possible that Neville had also had a problem, wasn't it?

I sighed. I had to find out. I was a detective now, or, at least, that was what Neville was paying me to be. I couldn't give up at this point. This was likely my last chance of doing something right. So now it was time to put my grey cells to work, as they said. Put those pieces together. Find that jar of pennies. Come out with something new.

I flipped through the photos again. That shining green hip flask seemed familiar. It wasn't in any of the other photos, but I had definitely seen it somewhere else. It might be important; since Jake Scott had apparently been sacked from the show for his alcohol problem, it seemed like the flask might hold an important key to the mystery.

I took the picture where Scott was having a meal. He was drinking water in that one. The size of the glass and the amount of liquid in it suggested water, not vodka; even if Scott had a drinking problem, that much straight vodka seemed a bit much. So, I had a man

126

having lunch at a Scotland pub, and he orders a glass of water to drink along with his meal. Not juice, not soda, but water. He seemed very sober while eating. I tried to get a grip on myself, saying that alcoholics drink water too, but something told me there was something else going on in there.

Okay, forget the flask. What else could mean something?

I put both pictures side by side. Jake Scott eating alone, Jake Scott playing chess. Jake Scott drinking water with a serious face. Jake Scott laughing while playing chess. Jake Scott wearing gloves and a scarf, Jake Scott with bare hands and neck...

I wished I had a magnifier, just to feel more like a detective, but I had to look at it with my bare eyes. In the first photo, as he had lunch not far from a lit fireplace, Jake Scott was much more warmly dressed than in the other picture. I picked up that one, where he was outdoors playing chess with the cameraman. There was something very odd about that one, and it wasn't just the absence of the gloves and the scarf: he seemed to be much warmer and happier. It wasn't the clothes that warmed him up; it was the contents of that shiny, green metal flask. So he drank; so did lots of people. What was new was the fact that he hadn't been drinking before. If those two pictures had been taken on the same day, which his clothing seemed to suggest, it meant somebody had given Scott a drink.

I was so close, but couldn't figure out where to go next. Maybe it was time to be creative again. Try to see the full picture and develop things back from there. It had worked in the past; why not now?

Let's see, what if...

127

…what if Jake Scott was trying to kill Neville?

…what if Jake Scott jumped from the waterfall because he was trying to send a message through his own death, but ultimately failed?

…what if Jake Scott was a recovering alcoholic?

I jumped out of my chair, ran to my room and pulled a yellow plastic box from under my bed. I'd been collecting clippings of every mention of *The Baker Street Sleuth* I could find for years. I'd never quite got around to organising them, and now that was biting me in the arse. It took me more than an hour to find it. My room looked like a disaster zone, strewn with clippings from newspapers, magazines and TV guides. It was just an ordinary picture of Neville, taken at the moorlands where he was shooting *The Hound of the Baskervilles*. He wore the cape and hat and was looking towards the horizon, his face heroic. In his hand was the same green flask as in the photo with Scott and the unidentified man. That was his flask. He had gotten Scott drunk, which led to his resignation.

I hated myself for coming to that conclusion. I wanted to believe those flasks were sold by the dozen every day, were stocked by every John Lewis and Debenhams in the country. Anyone could have bought one, I tried to reason. Jake Scott might have bought himself a green flask or borrowed it from another member of the crew. There was no reason to believe that Neville had purposefully sabotaged Scott, getting him drunk so he'd get fired on account of his behaviour. Was there?

I put down the photo and sighed. My first impulse was to call Lucy, but I managed to get a grip on myself. Beside the fact that he was a prima donna who didn't want to share the screen equally with

Watson, why would he want to ruin their careers? Could there be another reason — maybe the same reason he was killing the Watsons one by one?

I replaced the materials in the briefcase, shut it and put it back under my bed, next to my yellow box of clippings. Needing a drink, I went to the liquor store at the end of the street to buy some food and a bottle of vodka with the money Neville had given me. One thought wouldn't leave my head. I had to find Jake Scott. I had to talk to him before anyone else did.

But then what? Getting him to the police would be the smart thing to do. But it would be better if I went to them with the case closed. Then they would see how good I was. But how could I find a man who could be anywhere?

Neville was trying to find him in theatres and TV studios. I had to do something different.

A street kid passed by me, sniffling into an old handkerchief. He made eye contact with me for a second, and as he passed by my side he tried to grab my wallet from my pocket and run. I grabbed him by the hand and held him before he could run away. It could be just another thing to ruin what was left of my day, but my mind made the connection in a millisecond. The Baker Street Irregulars. The street kids that helped Sherlock Holmes in his investigations by gathering the information he couldn't get through the usual ways.

"What's your name, kid?" I said, still holding him.

"Are you joking?" he asked.

"I can give you far more than you'll get if you stab me and take my wallet."

The kid was reaching for his pocket knife, but seemed at the very least curious about my proposition. I knew it was a shot in the dark. The Irregulars would work much better in Victorian England than now, but I was starting to get really desperate. I could use some help finding Jake Scott. Neville would be looking for him in theatres and studios. Maybe I'd have a better luck looking elsewhere.

"I have a job for you," I said. "For you and for all of your friends."

"Are you a fag, mate?" he said, getting rid of my hand. He could have run away, but stayed put to listen to what I had to say.

"I need you to help me find a man," I said. "A guy who may or may not be on the streets."

He was paying attention. "Why don't you hire a detective?"

"I *am* a detective." It sounded really pathetic. But he was still listening, so I went on.

CHAPTER FOUR

The Flaw

As I entered my house, vodka in hand, a fist came out of nowhere and connected with my stomach. I doubled over in pain, the bottle slipping from my hand; Scorsese, with astonishingly quick reflexes, caught the bottle before it hit the ground. He set it aside and pulled me upright by my ear and, as I struggled to breathe through the pain, hauled me across the flat to the couch and then vanished into the kitchen. Bill was sitting in my armchair, the floor around his feet littered with peanut shells. I was starting to think I should invest in deadbolts.

"You don't listen very well, Mr Bellamy," he said, popping another peanut into his mouth. "I thought we agreed you weren't going to talk to your sweetheart or Neville about our little adventure."

I stared at a crease in the leg of his trousers, unwilling to meet his eyes. "I figured I'd never see you guys again," I said. "Figured you were a bad dream, or a really bizarre plot twist."

"You keep thinking in terms of fiction," he said, a note of amusement in his voice. "Let's talk real business now," he said. "Here's what we're going to do. As a show of good faith, I'm going to give you some more information, and trust that you're not going to make the same mistakes you did the last time."

'I can't make any promises,' I thought, but didn't say so out loud. I didn't have much leverage, and decided to listen. "Go on," I said. It wasn't like I had much of a choice.

"So here's the way I see it" Bill said. "You're currently hunting a man who may have a big secret, and you're on the right track." He leaned back in the armchair and crossed one leg over the other. "By the way, I caught an airing of *The Baker Street Sleuth* last night."

Forgetting myself momentarily, I asked eagerly, "What did you think of it?"

He gave me a look that said I was trying his patience, and then said, "I found it more entertaining than expected, actually." He paused before adding, "The reason I bring it up is because it was an episode where Holmes has to track down an incriminatory letter."

"*A Scandal in Bohemia*," I said. "Classic Holmes."

He made a noncommittal noise. "That episode got me thinking," he said. "About how smart our guy can be." "He's no real life Sherlock Holmes, I can tell you that."

He waved a hand dismissively. "I know that. I'm talking about this invisible villain we're going after. You see, just like Irene Adler, this enemy of ours has a secret that he wants to spread. He'd just have to find a way to spread it. And the best way to do it is being on national television." "And what kind of secret are we talking about?" I said.

"It's a code. A few words uttered at the right moment and in the right way. It wouldn't mean much for the general public, but there are some people who could use it. That's all I can tell you without revealing who my employers are." He steepled his fingers. "Here's what we know. Someone's trying to bring this secret out into the open. We think your actor friend is desperate to keep that secret

132

buried, but we're not sure. Same for your ginger girlfriend." He sighed. "We're wallowing in speculation at the moment."

There was a little voice at the back of my head complaining that this wasn't clarifying matters at all, only confusing them further, but I ignored it, more interested in pursuing my detective work.

"What do you want me to do?" "Keep on looking for Jake Scott," he said. "Start compiling a report. Next time we drop in, I'd like to be updated on the search." He studied me, and then said, "That's your first job. You might not like the second one so much."

"How bad can it be?"

He snorted. "We want you to keep an eye on the ginger and the actor. Compile another report for us on their activities. And for god's sake, man, stop letting yourself be jerked around like a puppet by the people around you. It's time for you to start pulling the strings yourself." "I'm a spy as well as a detective." I drank all my vodka at once. "But there's something else I want to know."

He glanced at his watch. "Keep it short," he said. "It's my daughter's birthday and I have to stop by Debenhams to pick up her present." "You keep talking about this big secret, and keep saying you can't say what it is. Do you even know what the secret is, or are you as in the dark as I am?" He stared at me for a long time, his eyes cold and distant. I couldn't make him answer the question, and I knew that if he didn't want to answer he wouldn't. I'd never felt so helpless in my own home before. I was worried too much to even get up to get more vodka, though I could really have used another drink. I didn't really think he'd do it, but I was distinctly aware that if he decided to rip my heart out with his bare hands that I was pretty powerless to stop him. It was a depressing thought to realise that at any moment Bill could just get up and walk away, and I'd be no further than where I'd started. I had zero leverage and even less power.

But there was something in his eyes, I thought, maybe a grudging respect — like he thought my efforts, everything I had gone through and was still going through, gave me the right to know at least something about what was going on. I hesitated to call that gleam in his eyes a vestige of humanity, but I didn't know what else to call it, either. As I stared at Bill, waiting for him to say something, he picked up his glass of vodka. I realised that this was the first time he'd touched it.

Bill lifted his cup in a silent toast and knocked it back again. "Jerry," he said, setting the mug down gently on the table, "I'm going to say a few words. Just enough to give you a vague idea of what's at stake. They probably won't help you much. You won't be able to do much with them. But you listen to me," he said, leaning forward, his eyes capturing mine, "and you listen hard. If any of what I'm about to say gets repeated, if any of it makes its way back to Neville or your ginger bitch, I swear to God that you'll be begging for the sweet release of death before I'm through with you. If that doesn't frighten you enough, let me add this: no one will be safe. Before you die, each and every single person you know — your parents, your brother and his family, the ginger — will suffer through unspeakable torture, because you didn't have the wit to stay silent when told. Don't talk to a shrink, don't talk to a priest, and most of all don't say a word to your whore or your idol. The pain will be everlasting and your death will be slow to come." His face drew near mine, and as he spoke, I could smell the vodka on his breath. "Do you understand?

134

"Y — yes," I said, trying to keep my hands from shaking. "I understand."

He meant it, and it terrified me.

"Good." Bill sat back in the chair again. "My client is involved in a war. Most of his profits come from the security industry, and he has developed some of this country's best security systems, that serve thousands, maybe millions of people." He paused dramatically and stared into his empty glass for a few seconds. "They are all based on an algorithm he believed to be flawless. A few years ago, somebody found a major flaw in that algorithm. Something that could make his clients' lives a living hell."

I nodded. The whole thing was a bit scary. "Go on."

"The first thing my client thought of was making drastic changes to his systems. But he can't do that without compromising his company. Also, he doesn't know yet what that flaw is."

"You're saying somebody wants to go to on national TV and spread that flaw?"

"A code, yes," Bill said. "And who knows who could decipher that code? From house burglars to international terrorists. I don't like it, you don't like it, but that's how things go, so why shouldn't people make a profit out of it?"

That little speech hadn't been rehearsed.

"But where there is a war," he continued, "there are sides. And that means that there are always men who haven't picked a side, who are willing to sell secrets to whichever side is willing to pay the most." Bill's eyes were on the empty glass in his hand, like he was talking to the last drops of vodka before they evaporated. "Do you get the picture?"

"I think so," I said. "And who do you think has that secret? Neville? Lucy? The next Watson?"

"Could be any of them." His expression was grim. "And he probably doesn't even know it. That's the worst part of it. Otherwise, we could just have that person killed — and trust me, we would do that. But my client is not willing to spill innocent blood until we've tried everything." He met my eyes again. "This makes it critical that we find who knows that, and quickly."

He took a piece of paper and a pen from his pocket and wrote down a phone number. Handing it to me, he said, "If you need to contact me for something important — I mean *really* important — use this number." He stood, setting the glass on the table, and said, "That's us off now. Keep your eyes open, kid, and here's hoping you've got something for me the next time we meet."

He went through the door, and Scorsese followed him. I kept staring at the floor, trying to figure out what to do next. I decided to find the next Watson by myself. But before that, I really needed a drink.

CHAPTER FIVE

Another Rock in a Rocky Way

The phone rang about four in the morning, but I answered it without questioning. It was Lucy.

"Hi, Jerry." Her voice was tired and hoarse.

"Are you all right?" I asked her.

"I've spent some quality time with a bottle. Nothing that won't go away by morning."

I checked the time. "It's almost morning. Do you want to meet?"

"I don't think that's a good idea. I...I just wanted to hear your voice and..."

She hung up. I almost called her back, but upon reflection it didn't seem like such a good idea. If she really had something important to tell me, she'd let me know. Given how confusing things had been lately, I wasn't sure that anyone really knew anything about anything anymore. Sure, Lucy had her problems, but I doubted they were worse than mine.

Right now, though, all I wanted to do was to go to the greasy café for the most gigantic breakfast in human history, so I slipped my keys into my pocket and headed out.

I felt really dizzy as I walked down the stairs, but kept walking. There were only a few people on the streets, but I still felt like I was in a really crowded place. When I realised how bad it was, it was too late. All I could do was bend down, trying to throw up. A woman passed by without looking at me. Well, in her place I'd do the same.

The life of a TV detective wasn't easy, and I was starting to understand that. For a guy who only ate crap and whose only daily exercise was masturbating in the shower, the shock was inevitable. I had to keep that in mind if I was going to continue in this line of work. I needed some food, some rest and some time to think things over, or else I would end up killing myself.

I fainted as I tried to get back home, and not a single soul thought of calling an ambulance. I don't know how much time I spent lying there in the gutter, but when I woke up somebody had already stolen my wallet, taking my documents, credit cards and the money I had left.

I looked around, hoping the thief would still be around. He could be on the other side of town, for all I knew. My head hurt and I was hungrier than I'd ever been before, but could at least stand up and walk. I made my way back home and threw myself on the couch, ready for some real sleep.

The phone rang as I closed my eyes, and this time it was Neville.

"How are you, dear boy?"

"What's the name of that feeling of being run over by a buffalo?"

Neville ignored me and said, "I got a visit this morning from Lewis Thompson's niece, Amanda. She sounded nervous. Said she had to leave the country immediately."

"Why would she call you?"

138

"She said you promised her some money, and wanted it in advance. It wasn't easy to convince her I couldn't pay her at the moment."

"Sorry for that," I said.

"But she did drop off her uncle's memoir," he continued, "and I can safely say two things. First, we're on the right track: there is a killer going after the Watsons. Thompson knew it; he'd received death threats himself. Second, he wasn't the Watson the killer was looking for…but he was pretty sure he knew who the killer was."

"Yeah, right," I said. "Listen, I'm tired and I'm hungry — any chance I could get some cash?"

"What happened to what I gave you? Did you drink it?"

"Some of it. And then I got mugged, so, you know, I'm skint again." I stared blankly at the wall and added, "I also hired some kids to find out stuff about Jake Scott, and when they turn up I gotta have something to pay them with."

"Right," Neville said. "Give me your address. I'll be there before lunch with Thompson's memoir. Try to get some rest."

I threw myself on the couch again after hanging up with Neville and tried to sleep, but even the gutter felt cosier. I wanted Lucy so badly that I couldn't get my body to relax. If only I could have felt the heat of Lucy's body, and heard her voice whispering in my ear — then maybe I could have got some rest. As tempting as it was, though, I couldn't call her. My day was messy enough as it was.

Knock, knock!

139

I dragged myself off the couch and went to the door. Three little juvenile offenders stared up at me, full of information and hungry for some cash.

"We got something for you," said Jimmy, the kid I had talked to the previous night. "You got something for us?"

I didn't have anything for them, but didn't want to let them know that. I had hoped that Neville would appear before the Irregulars, but no such luck.

They didn't ask for permission to come inside. Before I had the chance to say anything, they threw themselves on my couch. "This is a shitty place," said the tallest kid, who, judging from his appearance, probably lived somewhere nicer than my flat, like a cardboard box. He sounded disappointed. "From what Jimmy told us, we figured yours'd make a prime mark." It took me a minute to realise he meant they'd thought I'd have a good place to plunder. "There's nothing to rob here, except for a bunch of memorabilia," I said. "Can I get you lads some vodka?"

They all accepted. We sat down on the couch and I waited for them to begin.

"This man you're looking for," said Jimmy. "He lives under Pie Maker Bridge in Chelsea. They call him the TV man, because all he ever talks about is how he was on television a long time ago."

"We never saw him before," said the youngest one. "On TV, I mean."

"Said his name is Scott, same name you gave us," said Jimmy "The old sissy started crying when we showed him the pictures."

The kids laughed. I smiled and poured out another finger of vodka for each of them as encouragement. "He says he'd be willing to talk to you, mate, but he don't want to see the other guy, the tall one, you know? From the picture."

"Scott said if he sees that son of a bitch, he'll break the guy's spine with his bare hands." The kid shrugged. "His words, not mine."

Good news at last. I finally had a way to contact Watson number four, and if I was very, very lucky, I might even get to him before the killer.

"Did he ask who wanted to know? What did you tell him about me?"

"Everything you asked. Said you was an old friend of his, said you'd heard he'd been on the dole and thought you'd reach out a helpin' hand." He sniggered. "Think the idiot fell for it." He gave me a knowing look, and added, "We didn't tell him you was a fag, if that's what you're wantin' to know." "I'm not a... I'm not homosexual."

"You can be anything you like," the kid said. "It's not our concern. Where's our money?"

I'd known the question was coming, but had no satisfying answer for it. The kids had their hands in their pockets, and I bet their fingers were stroking pocket knives under the cloth. The only thing I had to maybe buy them off with was the bottle of vodka, but that wasn't really any kind of leverage.

"The money is in my room," I said. "Let me get it for you."

"We'll come along," said the taller one. "Just to make sure."

141

"I assure you I'm not lying," I said, in an incredibly unconvincing voice. "And I don't like having accusations thrown at me in my own home.

"Your own home!" Jimmy mocked "Yeah, lots to be proud of in this shithole, mate."

"Watch your mouth, kid," I said.

He met my eyes. "Don't you call me a kid again."

"I'm gonna go to my room," I said, thinking fast, "grab your money, and when I come back down we'll all have another drink before we go our separate ways." I folded my arms over my chest in an attempt to look intimidating. "And you don't accuse me of wrongdoing in my own house ever again."

Jimmy pulled his blade and pointed it at my stomach. The other kids followed suit.

"Don't test us, mate," he said. "We know where you live and we know how to get in and out of your house, probably better than you do. You go in that room, we go with you, and you give us all the money you got in this shithole you call a home. You do that, and we promise not to come back and slit your throat while you sleep." He grinned. "And if you try to run, we might pay another visit to your friend the TV man and see if his blood still runs red." He meant it. From the moment they'd entered the house, the kids had no intention of taking just what I'd offered them for the gig. And now I was stuck, staring down a knife and imagining myself bleeding out. So okay, I'd give them all my valuables and we could call it even — except for the part where I owned absolutely nothing of any value.

"Okay," I said at last. "You're right. I don't have the money. At least, not here with me."

Three sharp blades inched closer to my belly.

"So you're saying you lied to us?" asked the tall one, and he seemed to be almost rooting for that. It might mean they'd get to spill some blood — my blood.

"The money is with a friend of mine," I said. "If you let me make a call, I can get the money. I can even get extra for you."

Two blades went a little back. The tall kid's stayed where it was.

"You know what I think?" he said "I think you're full of shit. Give me one good reason not to spill your guts right now."

My eyes moved from kid to kid, trying to think of something I could use against them. At first sight, just your ordinary teenage delinquents. They smelled like sour beer and tobacco, but then I realised that the tall kid had a few dark spots on the tips of his fingers. He was the only one. Added to that, he had a thin pubescent moustache that seemed a little burned, and...

"You smoke like a girl, don't you?"

He lowered the knife quite a bit at that, enough for me to safely take a step aside.

"You like to smoke on your own," I said, slipping into my role as sleuth. "You don't smoke with the other kids, because you don't like to inhale. You have to pick up cigarette butts and smoke in a corner. Because you cough like a girl when you smoke, don't you?"

He'd dropped his guard. I had taken him by surprise, but I didn't think that was likely to last. But it didn't have to.

I grabbed the heaviest thing I could find — ironically an ashtray — and threw it at the tall kid, catching him between the eyes. He fell back, unconscious, and I ran out of the house while the others were still too surprised to follow. I ran until I couldn't run anymore, fell on my knees and nearly blacked out again. Once I'd recovered, I went to the first phone booth I could find and called Lucy. We had to save Jake Scott before those kids had a chance to reach him.

CHAPTER SIX

Finding Our Watson

Judging by the expression on her face, Lucy was ready to read me a sermon when she pulled over her car and opened the door for me. But she saw something that made the imminent tongue-lashing pause before it spilled over. I wasn't sure if it was the sense of urgency on my face or the fact I was as beaten up as an old tomato, but her hands flew to her mouth and she stared at me like I was a zombie.

"Jesus, Jerry, what happened to you?"

I slid into the car. "No time for explanations, honey," I said. "We got to get to Pie Maker Bridge as quickly as possible."

"Chelsea, right?" she said, pulling back out into the road.

"Yeah," I said. "And step on it!"

And so she did. I tried to explain to her as much as I could what had happened, but unfortunately there was no way of doing so without revealing we were going to find the fourth Watson. I'd have avoided it if I could as telling her would mess up my plans, but it was an emergency. I also told her about Thompson's funeral, leaving out the memoir affair. I told her about those brats who were trashing my house at that very moment, and Lucy suggested stopping the car, finding a phone booth and calling the police. Granted, they could be burning down my building along with everything I owned. She must have insisted on that, but I couldn't hear her. All I cared about was that we had found our Watson and we needed to get to him as quickly as possible.

It took us a while to find Pie Maker Bridge. It passed over an abandoned yard in which at least a dozen hobos had made their home, using sidings and asbestos to build ramshackle shelters. I was sure that Scott had to be down there, but as Lucy and I approached the nearest of the men, I had a bad feeling that it wasn't going to be as easy as picking him out of a crowd.

"Jake Scott!" I shouted. "I need to talk to Jake Scott!"

The men eyed me warily.

"No Scott here," said one at last.

"Where is he?" I demanded. Lucy shifted beside me, and I patted her arm to reassure her that I knew what I was doing. "I need to talk to him."

A big man came up to me, a piece of brick in his hand. I stared at it for a moment, uncertain if he meant to bash my head in with it or eat it for breakfast.

"You deaf, mate?" he asked, tossing the brick from one hand to the other. "There ain't no Scott here."

"We better go," said Lucy. "We'll get into trouble."

"I can handle this," I said.

"I don't think you can," she answered, very frankly.

My patience was running out. I'd been told Scott was here, and after everything I had gone through to save his miserable life, the least that he could do was announce himself and get in the car. And now Lucy thought I was a wimp. I decided to show what I could do.

"Listen," I said aggressively to the man with the brick, "I frankly don't give a damn about your ability to toss a brick back and forth. I'm looking for Jake Scott, and no dumb hobo with the IQ of a rock is going to stand in my way."

He flung the brick against a concrete pillar a few feet away; it shattered, and as I was staring at the cloud of brick dust, he held out his hands. "You think I need a brick to break your neck?" he inquired, cracking his knuckles.

"You don't give me Jake Scott, I'll be breaking your neck," I said. "I'm going to kick your face so hard your next incarnation will be the Elephant Man."

As I clenched my fists and tried to stare the giant down, it occurred to me that I might actually have to fight this guy — and I wasn't likely to be able to walk away on my own two feet. Lucy, happily, was better at being a diplomat than I was.

"Please, gentlemen," she said, stepping between us and resting a hand on each of our chests. "All my friend wants is to find Jake Scott." She smiled prettily. "Surely we can do so without bloodshed!"

The giant and I both opened our mouths, but Lucy spoke before either of us said anything.

"It doesn't matter who started it, and I don't want to hear any excuses. I'm finishing it." She looked from one of us to the other. "Can you two please make peace so we can get this over with?"

I shook hands with the big guy. Lucy smiled.

"Now," she said, "can any of you give us any information on Jake Scott?"

"Over here!"

Lucy and I turned to see an old man at the other corner of the factory yard, standing by a shack that looked in imminent danger of collapsing.

"I can help you," he said.

I wished I could run to him, but all my energy had drained away and I could barely walk. Lucy took me by the hand.

"Why did they listen to you?" I asked.

"You acted like you were better than they were," she said. "Like they owed you something. I treated them like equals. "

"Oh," I said.

The old man let us into his shack; with all three of us inside, it was cramped.

"Some kids were here this morning," said the old man. "Looking for Jake Scott. Funny thing, really. No one's looked for me in twenty years, and then twice in one day I get visitors."

"It's not safe for you to stay here," I said. "It would be best for you to come with us."

He raised his eyebrows. "What do you mean, it's not safe? I've lived here for six years and have seen all manner of people come and go in that time — drug addicts, rapists, prostitutes, pimps… What makes it suddenly so unsafe for me?"

148

"We have reasons to believe someone is trying to kill you because of your work in *The Baker Street Sleuth*."

Scott was looking at Lucy. She picked up his hand and met his eyes.

"We'll explain everything in time," she said, "but right now you really do need to come with us. It's not safe for us here, either."

That did the trick.

"Okay," said Scott at last. "I'll come, but not because of him." He jerked his head in my direction. "I don't trust him; kid doesn't seem in his right mind."

Lucy patted his hand. "He's just been through a lot," she said. "He's actually a very nice guy, but he's not so good at putting things in the right place." She leaned closer to him. "He can be quite selfish, you know, and he's not real good at figuring out who his real friends are…"

"That's enough!" I said, annoyed. "What is this, a shrink session? We're in a hurry, Lucy!"

"You're right," she said, looking sheepish. "We got to run."

Jake Scott put a few things inside a bag and we ran to Lucy's car. Once in the car, we realised we had another problem: where to now?

"We can eliminate my house from the list," I said. "Bloody everybody knows where I live."

Scott laughed. I didn't blame him. Even he was richer than I was.

"We should go to the police," Lucy said.

"We should. But can we?" I asked. "How would we explain everything? Where would we begin?"

"We'll have to do it eventually," she said quietly.

Lucy was probably right, but then she hadn't gone through as much as I had. She had no idea the kind of pain that was headed our way. Going to the cops might seem like the easy way, but I knew it wasn't the best course of action. Thinking back, it was amazing how many excuses I made every time somebody suggested calling the police. It was like they were going to ruin all the fun of it.

With that in mind, I said, "What about your vengeance? Don't you want Neville's head?" Even as I said it I felt guilty.

Jake Scott grabbed my shoulder from the back seat, so tight I almost yelled.

"Neville?" He spoke the word with disgust and a bit of disbelief. "Bart Neville?"

"Yeah," Lucy said, sounding even more disgusted. "Did he ruin your life as well?"

He told us his story, which was more or less as I had deduced. During the shooting of *The Final Problem*, Neville had convinced Scott to have a couple of drinks during the breakouts. Scott had been sober for more than seven years at the time. He got so drunk he tried the stunt with the waterfall and almost died. Nobody would listen to him. Eventually the drinking ended his marriage, and he'd been working on putting his life back together since then.

"You should have seen me act when I was sober," he said, tears in his eyes. "I know most people think I'm a big ham, but I used to be

150

good. After I was fired from *The Baker Street Sleuth*, I started to go to the meetings again, but it was useless. I wake up in the morning and the first thing I do is have a drink. I go through at least a bottle a day."

That was all very touching, but what I really wanted to know was if Scott was the Watson we (that is, the killer and I) were looking for. The one who knew the secret, whatever it was.

"Let's find a hotel," Lucy said.

"Can't we go to your place?" I asked.

"No!" she said. "You think I want to bring all this home with me?"

We found ourselves a bed and breakfast nearby, and Lucy paid for a room with two beds. It was much nicer than what we were used to. Scott took the opportunity to have a long shower, leaving me and Lucy to discuss the situation.

I was hungry. "Can we order breakfast?"

"It's one in the afternoon, Jerry," she said.

"Can we order lunch, then?"

She sighed. "I really don't care. Look, Jerry, I have a life, and you're not letting me live it."

"Listen, Lucy," I said, more seriously. "Someone's trying to kill Scott, but aside from that none of us know what's coming next. Seems to me that we could order some food and talk things over before it gets even more complicated. Trust me, it will."

She sat down next to me on the bed, looking concerned, and took my hands. Scott came out of the bathroom, dressed in a white robe, his beard clean. He looked much more like a human being now. He sat on the other bed with a serious look and asked us to explain what was going on. He wanted to know everything from the start. Lucy and I looked at each, completely hopeless about where to start.

CHAPTER SEVEN

A Quest for Sugar

As a kid, I liked to follow ants. It amazed me the way they were always able to find sugar, even in places they'd never visited before. I usually never saw ants on my desk, but if I left a little bit of sugar on it and waited a day, they appeared by the hundreds. I started to spread sugar around the house and follow the ants that came from the anthill. In doing so, I realised that they didn't come looking for sugar, but that the sugar looked for them. The ants walked around without thinking about sugar, because they knew in their hearts that there was sugar in their future.

Sometimes I felt like that. It was like this whole case was going in my direction, and that if I just kept walking, the truth would eventually come along. The thing was, I didn't want to sit on my butt waiting for the mountain to come. It wasn't in my nature.

Lucy left me with Scott at the B&B, and even though I could have used a few hours of sleep, my mind was too busy to rest. Scott was very thankful for the chance to sleep in a nice bed, and snored like a chainsaw. I really wished he'd wake up so we could talk about things.

As soon as Lucy left, I picked up the room phone and called Neville. He didn't answer so I rang back every ten minutes until he finally picked up — three hours later.

He sounded really pissed when he answered the phone. "Where the hell are you?" he demanded. "I just came from your house and it's a ruddy mess."

"It's a long story."

"It's always a long story, isn't it? Where are you?"

"I'm at a B&B. Do you still have the memoir?"

"Yeah. I need your help. Where are you? Shall I come to you?"

Bad idea. "I'll come to yours," I said. "I'll be there as soon as possible."

Lucy gave me some money to order a pizza, but I was a long way past being both hungry and tired. I was in a bizarre state of mind; my brain didn't seem to be attached to my body. I took a long shower and then sat on the bed and stared at the walls for a long time, thinking. Just like sugar to ants, the answers should start coming at any time. Why shouldn't there be answers right there, in that room that I shared with Scott? Maybe it was time to start finding those answers, or at least to try. I couldn't leave the room for now, but they say there everywhere you look there is something to be found. So I looked at the floor, I looked at the beds, I looked at the small TV, I looked at Jake Scott, who was having the best nap of his entire life. I got up and walked around the room, looking at every corner, until there was no place to look. The sugar wasn't in that room. It wasn't that simple. Or maybe I wasn't being a good ant.

The phone rang.

"Mr. Smith, this is the front desk. I just wanted to inform you that a man came looking for you."

It was the receptionist. Lucy had offered to grease his palm so if something like this happened, he'd call us before calling the police.

"What man?" I asked.

"A very tall man, sir. He said he was looking for a man with your appearance, followed by a redhead woman and a…an older man."

The tall man. Shit.

"Did you tell him…"

"I didn't tell anything sir, as it's against our policy to give out information like that. But I believe you should…"

I hung up. My first impulse was to wake up Scott so we could get the hell out of there, but I realised Lucy needed to know what was going on. I picked up the phone and dialled her number, but she didn't pick up. I called three times, but nothing. Well, she could be anywhere right now, couldn't she? And if there was somebody after her, she had that panic button of hers. I had to stay calm and figure out a plan for when she came back.

Somebody knocked at the door. I grabbed the lamp from the bedside table to use as a makeshift weapon and unlocked the door, prepared to bash the tall man in the head.

But it wasn't him. It was Lucy. Her left eye was black, her neck was bruised and she was limping, favouring her left leg.

"Jerry, I…"

And then she fell on the floor. I picked her up, set her on the bed, and nudged Scott awake. He sat bolt upright, and had just opened his mouth to say something — probably to complain — when he saw Lucy sprawled on the bed. That made him put himself together in a millisecond.

"Oh, my god, what happened?" he asked. He had grown quite fond of Lucy in those few moments they had spent together, probably because she'd been the first person in years who'd actually treated him as a human being. When she first left, he wanted to go with her, but Lucy said she had to be alone for a while. At that moment I wished he'd insisted.

"The man…" Lucy whispered.

"The tall man?" I asked.

She nodded and closed her eye in pain.

"I was at home," she said, "and he got me… He took a lot out of me, Jerry… We have to run…"

"Why didn't you…" I asked.

"My car is…outside," she said, without letting me finish. "The keys…are in the ignition."

"That's good," I said. "We'll get you to hospital."

"Jerry…you'll have to carry me."

Scott peered outside, making sure nobody was watching, and then between the two of us we got Lucy to the car. We put her in the back seat and I slid behind the wheel. As we drove away, Scott kept an eye on the mirrors to make sure no one was following us, but I didn't trust him: his hands were shaking, and I was afraid that instead of focusing on the more immediate concern that his thoughts were on how and when he'd get his next drink.

"You need to see a doctor" I said over my shoulder, watching Lucy in the rear-view mirror. Her purse was on the passenger seat, and the panic button had fallen on the ground. I bent over and picked it up, not sure if I should press it. Lucy said something, but I didn't hear her, because something inside my head suddenly clicked into place.

"We have to go back," I said abruptly.

"Go back where?" she asked.

"We have to go back to the B&B!" I said. "There's something in the room that I need to see again."

"What are you talking about?"

I made an illegal U-turn and headed back to the B&B. Lucy was talking rapidly, trying to get my attention; beside me, Scott seemed too dazed to understand what was happening.

I tried not to think too hard about what I was doing, since it was incredibly risky and stupid and with both Lucy and Scott with me, I really shouldn't have been going back. But if I'd had a choice, I wouldn't have gone back — it was just that there was something we'd left behind in that room that I was sure was the key to solving the case.

I parked just in front of the door and ran in, leaving Lucy and Scott behind me in the car. Ignoring their shouts, I investigated every possible corner in the room, trying to find the thing that had made everything click into place in my mind. Where could it be?

Then I heard a shot. And a scream. A car door slammed and I heard an engine turn over before tires squealed.

When I got back outside, Lucy's car was gone, and so was Lucy. Jake Scott's body was lying on the asphalt. I dashed back into the room and dialled the number Bill had given me.

"What's the matter, Bellamy?"

"I'm going to give you an address," I said hurriedly, "and you need to be here before the police."

I told him the name of the B&B and hung up, fighting back despair. Lucy was gone and I hated to even imagine what could happen to her in the hands of the tall man. And then there was me, again failing in everything I tried to do. Why'd I have to come back to this place, anyway? What had I been hoping to accomplish?

My eyes caught a piece of white plastic on the ceiling. And then everything made sense. I was thrown back to the convention, the fire alarm and… Oh God!

I was about to shout eureka when a man in black grabbed me by the shoulder and pulled me outside, practically throwing me inside his car. As we went away, I had a smile on my face. Not even the thought of Lucy being in danger could wipe it off of my face.

CHAPTER EIGHT

This Lemon Pie is Killing Me

"You should eat something," said Bill, sounding concerned.

We were in an Italian restaurant that had apparently been shut down just for us. Bill had ordered me a huge spaghetti dish, but I hadn't touched it. My mind was too uneasy, and so was my stomach.

"You got to find Lucy," I said. "Her life is in danger."

"Don't worry," he said easily. "We'll find her. Tell me what you know."

For a moment it had seemed like the pieces of the puzzle had all been in the right place, and then we lost everything. But the image of that piece of plastic was clear in my head. Deep down I knew it was the key to that whole charade.

I took a deep breath and dove in. "We were all trying to figure out who had pushed the fire alarm button. At the convention, that is. Neville was about to answer Lucy's question about her father when the alarm went off, and the place had to be evacuated. We all agreed that it was someone who didn't want the world to know about the Watson killer, which is why we thought the killer himself did it. And, last but not least, we knew a woman had phoned the press and told them about the tall man." I paused for breath, and then continued.

"Somebody said something about the tall man, and after that we started to think of him as the killer. Someone had to have triggered the fire alarm; it seemed like he'd done it. The problem was," I said, really getting into the swing of things now, "how could one person listen to Lucy's question, realise what she was about to say, and then run to the hallway and push the button without being noticed? That seemed quite impossible. The person should have found a way to set the alarm off without leaving the room. But what if the button hadn't been pushed? What if the alarm went off for a different reason?"

He looked puzzled. "What do you mean?"

"Smoke detectors."

I actually enjoyed the look on his face. It was nice to impress a man who clearly had seen a lot in his time.

"It's a guess," I said, "but it is a damn good guess. If the theatre had smoke detectors, all it would take was somebody lighting a cigarette, and the game would be on. Everybody would conclude that that was what caused the alarm, and there would be nothing wrong with that. But somebody — *somebody* — wanted people to believe that a tall man was there. They wanted us to believe that a tall man *existed*."

Bill looked at the table for a while, then reached into his pocket for what I guessed was a pack of cigarettes, but stopped halfway and called the waiter around and ordered a pint of beer.

"When all this is over," he said to me, "I think I might hire you."

"If I was behind all this," I said. "I would certainly use it to put the police on the wrong track. If I were very tall, I wouldn't spread the word that there was a tall man involved. I would invent someone completely different to put them on the wrong track."

"But people have seen such man."

"Lucy told me a tall man had beaten her up. Neville said a tall man had been in his house. But our guy could have hired a tall man anywhere in London to do the job. But we are not looking for the tall man. We're looking for someone else: the brain behind all this."

He regarded me thoughtfully. "Do you have any theories?"

"I have one, and it's very good. But I need to clear up some points before telling you. I need help. One more thing, though. This morning, a tall man came looking for me at the B&B. We need to get to this guy."

He snapped his fingers and Scorsese appeared from behind a column. Bill gave him some orders and sent him away.

"We'll be taking care of that," he said. "What now?"

I rubbed my eyes with my palms.

"Why isn't everything being taken care of?" I asked. He raised his eyebrows. "Surely your department, whatever it is, should be able to get to the bottom of this mess more quickly than me."

The waiter reappeared with his beer. Bill waited until he was gone before answering my question.

"Remember what I told you about the war we are going through? The information war?" He took a sip and continued, "It's a very delicate business. If my people get into this, it could ruin everything. We've been wanting to put a man inside this scheme for some time, but we've always failed. Now that we have you, we need to use you."

"I knew I was being used." I scowled down at my spaghetti.

"Think of this as a sport. When you're watching a game and your team is losing, you can root for them, you can show some support. What you can't do is jump onto the field and kick the ball yourself. Me and my people, we're not inside the game. You are."

"Are you rooting for me, then?"

"Wholeheartedly." He smiled thinly and drank his beer.

"You got to tell me more. What kind of information we are going after?"

"It's most likely in code," he said. "A specific phrase spoken in a specific context. It could be something simple, like 'I like lemon pie' or 'my leg is killing me'. Most people wouldn't notice, but to the right people it could mean a hell of a lot."

I considered that. Four Watsons were dead, with one still to go: David Elroy, the actor who'd played the role in the dreadful last series. He was the last one alive, but as far as we knew, any one of the Watsons who were already dead could have possessed the secret.

"I've put some of my men out looking for this last Watson," Bill said, as though he could read my thoughts. "We haven't been able find him, at least not with our methods."

"So I guess I'll have to use mine."

"You found the last one before the killer did."

He was right about that. I had successfully found Jake Scott, using methods that would never have occurred to most people.

162

Unfortunately, once I'd got my hands on him, I'd let him sleep, and then the poor schmuck had ended up dead — and I didn't know any more than I had before I'd found him. Worse still, Lucy had fallen into the hands of the killer.

I hung my head. Guess I wasn't actually the best detective in business.

Scorsese came from the restaurant door with a remote control in his hand.

"Sir, I think you should see this."

There was a big TV on one of the walls. Sanderson turned it on and we saw Neville sitting by an ambulance, his head covered in bandages. A pretty reporter was talking to him.

"I'm here again with Sir Bartholomew Neville, an actor best known for his role as Sherlock Holmes in *The Baker Street Sleuth*. A few minutes ago, he was involved in an accident, and has refused to go to hospital." She leaned forward slightly and the camera zoomed in a bit. "According to Sir Bartholomew, this was no accident, but an attempt on his life."

She held the mic close to his face; he spoke slowly, tasting every word.

"I was driving back from my friend's place when a red car hit me," Neville said, staring directly at the camera. "On purpose. I almost died."

"Do you know who it was?" the reporter asked eagerly.

"Couldn't even tell you if it was a man or a woman," he said. "But there's someone out there who has it in for me — and I can tell you right now that I'm not his first victim."

The reporter's eyes lit up. "So, you're saying there's a killer on the loose? Are the police investigating?" She thrust the mic back into his face.

"There is definitely a killer out there," he said gravely. "My assistant and I are tracking this lunatic, and we're not going to let him get away with this."

"What about the police?" she demanded. "Are they involved? Do you think they'll let you continue your investigation?"

"They don't have to let me do anything," he said. "However..." He smiled, put his hand into his jacket pocket and pulled out an envelope. With the reporter waiting with bated breath, he removed a yellow piece of paper from the envelope and proudly displayed it to the camera. It was a private detective certificate with his name on it.

"In case you didn't know," he said, "I took Private Investigations course as part of my preparation as an actor, and I've just received a fresh copy of my certificate. Which means I'm allowed to investigate this case!"

We watched until the reporter returned the news to the anchorman. Neville had revealed a lot about the Watson killer to the news. Not everything, but quite a lot. More than I would have said, that's for sure.

"What do I do now?" I asked.

He shrugged "Your best shot is probably with him."

"With *him*?!" I asked. "I can't trust him anymore!"

"It's not a matter of trust, Jerry. He's is determined to get in the media with this crazy story, and that might be the best chance you have of finding a man who seems to have dropped off the face of the earth. Because now the killer is going to be more careful. He's not acting in the shadows anymore. Neville trusts you, and you can use that trust to find out a lot. The public will be on his side, and that's the worst thing that can happen to our killer."

"You want me to be him. The new Watson."

"You have to. He did mention an assistant in that interview, didn't he?"

That was right. It could be my only chance of getting Lucy back. I got up, leaving the spaghetti untouched, and went to the black sedan parked outside, where Sanderson was waiting to drive me to Neville's place. I kept thinking about her, and the smoke, and the way things were getting more and more difficult

CHAPTER NINE

From the Memoir of the Late Lewis Thompson

Neville wanted me to read the whole manuscript at his place, so we could start thinking about what to say to the press, but I talked him into letting me bring it home. It was already dark when the cab dropped me at my flat. The place was destroyed. Everything had either been broken or torn apart, and I guess I should thank Jimmy and his mates for not setting the whole place on fire. There were threats written on the walls and they had pissed all over my memorabilia. I lay as I could in what was left of my mattress and started reading.

Through the course of my not so joyful life, I have been a man of many obsessions. According to my parents, the only toy that kept me from crying as a baby was a red wood rattle. No other toy could entertain me; it didn't matter if it was prettier or more colourful. As a child, I was involved in a wide variety of sports, but never managed to find myself in any of them. We had a nice courtyard where I could bring my friends for soccer or basketball matches. We could kick and throw a ball, and afterwards we'd all crowd inside, tired and sweaty, and down the fresh-squeezed lemonade my mother had made.

But that soon became boring. Though I was a pretty good player, my interest for that kind of sport began to fade, to the point that I left the other kids playing by themselves and spent my time in the house, looking at the figures in an old book my dad kept in a drawer. The pictures showed a man in a white uniform, in the middle of a run. I spent hours looking at one particular photo, where he was about to cross the finish line. The look in his face was that of a man who had finally achieved his greatest goal in life.

"That's Roger Bannister," said my father to me. "World's greatest runner."

That was everything I needed to hear. I decided, at that point, that I was going to be the world's greatest runner. I became my own coach and started to run everywhere, as fast as I could. It didn't take long for me to become the best runner in the neighbourhood. Every conflict between me and another kid was settled by a race, and I always, always won.

And then the day arrived when that was no longer satisfactory, just as it had for every other sport I'd ever tried. Swimming, rugby, golf: they were all delightful until the day they were not. So I tried to find myself in other activities. Music, painting, books. They all lost their magic really fast. By the time I was fifteen, my parents had already acknowledged the fact that their son was going to go through life without finishing anything.

But then theatre came along, and it changed everything. When I started, there was nothing to make me think it was going to be different than anything else I'd occupied my time with over the years. I took my first classes and was amazed by the idea of becoming someone else, of creating someone else on the stage. It was a powerful idea. It was so fantastic that the idea of one day giving up such power was scary. Every night I prayed by my bed, asking God to help me continue acting.

He heard my prayers. A year went by, then another, and theatre was always fresh and new to my spirit. I did my first one-act play at the age of fifteen, and my first full-length play at seventeen. My parents were very supportive, especially considering what I heard from my colleagues, many of whom had parents terrified by the idea that their kids didn't want a regular job with a safe income.

But the truth was that the money wasn't always that good, and from time to time I needed to do different things to survive. Wish I could say they were always legal and righteous things, but that just wasn't always the case.

There were many ways of getting cash in those days. Though I've never put my hands on another man's possessions or pulled a trigger, there were some things an actor could do onstage that could get him a little bonus. I presented myself to hundreds of people every night, and from time to time a mysterious man came to my dressing room with a cheque and instructions for me to cough at certain points in the play, or stare at a specific place while saying a line. To the rest of the cast and crew the modification seemed like a simple improvisation, but according to the man with the cheque, I was delivering important information to someone in the crowd. It was a weird way of saying things, but he said there were many people that did the same, some of them maybe even in the same play as me. It was all about communication and power, he said. Secret communication and secret power.

There was only one fellow actor who I was positively assured was engaged in that kind of activity. We called him Mort, and he was a very discreet man and still a great actor. One day, after a couple of shots at a pub, Mort told me that he was starting to make his own business out of the passing of secrets. Coughing on stage was just the beginning, he said. Imagine how much we could earn with code information on radio, or TV! It was a world of possibilities, an invisible net around the world. He told me that a kidnapper could hold the life of a little girl in his hands at a given moment, with the radio playing by his side; if the next song was Pledging my Love, *he'd abort the mission. If it was* When Joanna Loved Me, *the girl would be pushing daisies in no time.*

"And trust me," he said. "The DJ is getting a lot of money!"

It all seemed too bogus to me, so I declined the offer to become his partner. Our lives went separate ways. For many years I was on the stage every weekend, just as I'd always dreamt. Never got to play Hamlet at the Old Vic, but then that was every actor's dream. But after a while, I couldn't delude myself any longer. It had been many years since I'd last heard anything about the information racket, but there were times where I had to make ends meet with jobs that I wasn't proud of. But pride was too expensive, and at the time I couldn't afford to be choosy.

And then, one day, my agent came to me, saying he'd got me a big role on a TV show. Now, television was never among my obsessions. But between doing what I loved for little and doing everything else for the money, I jumped at the chance.

Working on television turned out to be a nightmare, worse than anything I'd ever imagined. The shooting schedule was incredibly tight, meaning that there was hardly any time allowed for rehearsal. I knew I could act, but acting in front of that giant mechanical beast they called a camera, with all those people behind it, was too much for me. We shot most of scenes in the studio, for which I was grateful; filming on location would have been too much for me to handle.

That leads me to the show's protagonist. What is there to say about Bartholomew Neville that hasn't already been said?

Bartholomew Neville was the epitome of the phrase prima donna. He wasn't simply a spoiled star; the man had no muse but himself. He was always complaining about something: my expression, my delivery, my look, my voice, my tone… So many good shots were thrown away because he thought his hat wasn't right; so many writers were fired because he didn't like his lines. When I think now about how much money was spent due to his caprice…

The cash was good, I can't lie about that. It helped me to settle down, to put some meat on the table. But the money wasn't nearly enough to compensate for the crap that I put up with from that hideous man. I told myself that I wasn't going to go back to criminal activities to make money, that I just needed to grit my teeth and keep acting, but eventually I began to wonder if there was a way I could take advantage of my position.

Then one night I went to a play and Mort was up on the stage. Nothing big, just a bit part in a few scenes. We went out for a few drinks after the show and I told him about the series.

"I saw an episode or two," Mort said. "How do you like it?"

"I don't like it at all," I admitted. "To be quite frank, it's becoming unbearable. All I want is to go back to the theatre."

"You could quit," he suggested, and then laughed at the expression on my face before sobering. "Hate to tell you, mate, but things aren't that great in the theatre world, either."

"I know that," I told him. And I did. "But TV is so cold! There's no real interaction, no bond between the players, no reactions from the audience. It's all about making money."

He asked the barman to bring another couple of shots.

"So are you making much money, then?" he asked.

Over innumerable shots and long into the night, we talked. I was drunk enough to tell him how much I made and that I wanted to make even more, to keep from ever worrying about money again. At the end of the night, Mort gave me his card. He asked me to call when the money started to go short.

It didn't take long: two weeks later we were having coffee together.

"I have things that could be done on TV," he said. "We're talking about a lot of information here. People say that computers are the future, but it's nothing compared to the ability to send a message to one person hidden amongst millions."

"Tell me more."

"It's not much different from what you were doing a few years ago on the stage. Let's say I tell you to put your right hand on the table instead of your left one. That may mean a lot to a client of mine."

"Are we talking about criminals?" I wasn't sure how I felt about that, but then again, I'd never asked in the past.

"Criminals, not criminals, who cares? Do you know what the message is and who it's being delivered to? No. So what's the problem?" He shrugged. "It's just a code, and that code might mean a lot to people watching. We are talking about an invisible market, my friend, and that hand can mean anything." He laughed. "Plus, it's more people watching your shitty show."

He was convincing, and so I said yes. Soon I had more money in my bank account than I knew what to do with, because I was willing to perform a little gesture that — I kept telling myself — was harmless.

As he gained confidence in me, Mort told me a little more about the business.

"This is much more usual than you think," he said. "You've heard of TV reporters that give a little wink at the end of their stand-up, just as a nod to their children. Their kids at home know that that was just a little 'hello' from Mum or Dad, but the rest of the country doesn't pick up on the message. The code only means something when it's recognised by both the sender and the receiver: two people have to know how to decode it."

"Let's say I have photos that can compromise a particular person's status," he said. "They're not with me, but with a guy who knows the code. But what if the cops have bugged my phone? I can't call my friend and tell him to burn the incriminating photos; instead, I pay a guy to tell the newspaper reviser to print the word cake wrong, because that's the code."

"It sounds absurd," I said.

"It has to! That's the whole point. It's a bizarre market, and we own it. Believe me, our clients aren't street criminals or blackmailers. There are any number of very distinguished people needing our services."

171

"How high up does this go?" I asked. "The clients, I mean. How high up do they go?"

Mort laughed and patted me on the back.

"Keep on going as you've been going, and maybe one day you'll know."

And so I did. For the next three episodes of The Baker Street Sleuth, *I must have sent at least a dozen of those messages. The hardest part of it was doing it in every single take, because every scene was shot multiple times, and it wasn't until the material hit the cutting room floor that we'd know which version would make the final show. The worst thing that could happen was for me to pass the wrong message. It wasn't theatre, but then again, it wasn't supposed to be. It got easier with every take, and the cheques kept coming. My plan was to collect as much money as possible early so that later I could invest in my stage career and still live comfortably.*

But as the filming continued, it became clear to me that my work on the series wasn't going to last. Bartholomew Neville had made it clear that he didn't like me. He didn't like anyone on the set, but it had become increasingly obvious that he had a particularly hard time dealing with the actors playing Watson. I didn't care much for the role and I didn't much care for the show, but those secret messages I'd been sending had made me a fair amount of money, giving me an incentive to stick around. I was sure there had to be a way to take a little more advantage of that before the curtain fell down on me.

One day, just before getting sacked, I was talking to the casting directors. They were looking to cast a vital role for one of the next episodes: Professor James Moriarty, Sherlock Holmes' greatest enemy. Two actors had already been cast and had promptly quit after their first attempts to shoot scenes with Neville. They asked me if I knew anyone from theatre, someone with a thick skin who could endure the lead actor's attitude.

"I think I know someone," I told them. "His name is Jay Mortigan. We call him Mort."

I couldn't fall asleep after reading those words, so I went for a walk. Not able to afford a pint at a pub, I just wandered, trying to think about the case. After that turn of events, we finally had a villain in our little pulp story: Professor Moriarty himself, Jay Mortigan. It couldn't be more perfect. There was no way of escaping it now: Neville was Sherlock Holmes and I, his sixth Watson. In a way, that meant I was a potential victim as well. But that wasn't bothering me. All I could think about was Lucy. We had to save her.

It was a Saturday night, so there were plenty of people on the streets. As I walked by, they stared at me in a funny way, and I figured it was because I looked like a zombie. I couldn't sleep, couldn't eat and felt my whole body aching. It was only as I passed by an old parked truck and saw my reflection in the wing mirror that I realised there was something else.

Sure, I was much thinner and my eyes had huge bags under them. But that wasn't what caught my attention. The truth was that I looked much older, and not just because I was tired. I had this strange look in my eyes that made me look almost wise. It was like I was thirty years older, despite having the face and the body of a young adult, and that somehow was making people uncomfortable. I stared at the mirror for a long time and decided to go back home. The next days would be even harder for me.

PART THREE — A GAME OF PSEUDONYMS

CHAPTER ONE

Do You Think the Hat is Too Much?

He must have asked me something, and I should probably have paid attention to every word he said. But after everything that had happened, the words of Sir Bartholomew Neville weren't that important anymore. And to think that, a week ago, I would have done anything — and I do mean *anything* — just to kiss the soil his feet touched. But now, he was common. Worse than common: annoying. He had allowed me to sleep at his place, not because he was concerned about me, but because we had had to talk to the press first thing in the morning, and he didn't want to take any chances by leaving me on my own.

I was sitting on his couch, looking down at my hands, pretending there was a picture of Lucy there and wishing I could cry. The cops were already looking for her, and it was probably just a matter of time before they found her — it was just a matter of how many pieces she'd be in.

Neville was far from being as concerned as I was. The whole thing seemed to amuse him. I woke up to him wandering around the house, whistling *The Baker Street Sleuth* opening theme. God, I was starting to hate that show so much!

The whistling stopped, and Neville said: "I asked you a question."

I turned my eyes to Neville. He was wearing a three-piece tweed suit, with a matching cape and — I'm deadly serious — a deerstalker hat, the same one he'd worn when playing Sherlock Holmes.

"I beg your pardon?" I said, perplexed.

"The hat," he said, pointing to his head. "Do you think it's too much?"

"Do you really think it's a good idea to go to give an interview about a series of murders related to the image of Sherlock Holmes...dressed as Sherlock Holmes?"

"I don't see your point," he said.

I shrugged. "If I were going to talk to the cops about the Zodiac killer, I wouldn't wear a Saint Seiya t-shirt. Get rid of the hat. And the cape."

"Fine," he said sourly, sounding like a child who'd been denied a promised treat.

The press knew very little about Lucy, and I figured it was probably better that way. That interview would be a waste of precious time, but at this point there was no avoiding it. With any luck, they'd find the fifth Watson much more quickly than Neville and I. I didn't care about David Elroy. Finding Lucy was all that mattered to me now. And, surprisingly enough, I had a lead on Jay Mortigan.

It would have been much harder if Mortigan had faded into obscurity like the Watsons. He never got super famous or something like that, but did get some minor parts here and there. He'd never really completely lost contact with his fans until a couple of years ago, when he stopped appearing at conventions. Now that he had apparently quit the show business — probably to get a real job and start a real life — it wouldn't be easy to find him. I suspected that his real name wouldn't be Jay Mortigan, either — it just sounded too theatrical and too close to his *Baker Street Sleuth* character's name — but I might be able to find it with the help of my not so dear friend Caesar Ace He once got to interview Mortigan for his fanzine, *Calabash Smoke*, I don't know how, and liked to brag that he knew the location of his house. He would never tell it to anyone, saying that it wouldn't be ethical. We all had our doubts that he was telling the truth, but if he did know where to find Mortigan, I would get that information out of him.

At the moment, however, I was stuck with Neville. He'd told the police everything he knew about me, and as his supposed partner, I had to be by his side.

Thankfully, he didn't know that I'd been in the motel when Jake Scott was shot. Maybe he wouldn't have revealed that information if he'd known it, but one thing I'd figured out was that Neville had a few screws loose. To him, the spectacle, the performance, was more important than real life. I could at least rely on the fact that I wasn't a suspect in Scott's murder.

"I'm almost ready," Neville yelled from his room. He was taking forever to choose his cufflinks. I was wearing that same old suit, the only one I had. He gave another yell: "When we get there, you let me do the talking. I'm more accustomed to the press."

"I don't mind," I answered from the living room. "Just be careful."

"What do you mean?" he asked.

"You tend to give people too much information. I don't think it's a good idea, especially when we are talking to the press."

He didn't answer. I looked at my watch. Should I wait until we got back to make that call? I couldn't wait. Borrowing Neville's phone, I rang Ace. He picked up the phone on the first ring.

"Hello?" said the sleepy voice.

"I need a favour," I said.

"I'm sorry, who is this?" he asked, sounding confused.

"It's Jerry," I said.

"Bellamy? How'd you get my number?"

"Phonebook," I said. "Say, Ace, how'd you like to get your hands on the magnifying glass Neville used in *The Five Orange Pips*?"

"Please, let me sleep. I don't have time for your shit."

"Okay," I said. "But I know some people who'd be interested in it."

"Are you serious?" he asked. "How the hell did you acquire that piece?

"Long story," I said, feeling pretty pleased with the way things were going. "Look, you want it or not?"

"What's the catch?" he asked.

"I want Mortigan's address," I said.

He remained silent for half a minute, and then said: "Are you trying something funny?"

"If you don't believe me," I said, "you can have your half of the deal before you give me mine."

A brief silence followed. I could imagine the little wheels turning inside his head. I don't know what was worse to him: that I had such a valuable piece of memorabilia or that it meant so little to me that I was willingly to get ready of it for seemingly worthless information.

"I think I'll play along," he said, still dubious. "Just because I heard a few rumours about you, and if you really have what you say you have, it could confirm some of them."

"What kind of rumours?" I asked, a bit surprised.

"People say you started some crazy shit to get close to Neville. I'd like to know how crazy you got."

"You want to know how crazy am I?" I asked, infuriated. "Check tomorrow's newspapers." And then I hung up. That was one thing taken care of. Now I had to get used to the idea of appearing in the press. My role would be just a supporting one, but I also had to find a way of controlling Neville in front of the reporters without letting them notice.

"Shall we go?" Neville was standing by his door, wearing a grey business suit with a black tie and black shoes. And though he wasn't dressed as Sherlock Holmes anymore, the way he said those three words, the way he looked at me and, most of all, the haughty way he stood by that door, made me feel more than ever that I was in the presence of the Baker Street Sleuth.

"Yes," I said. "If we have to."

CHAPTER TWO

The Interview

I was expecting something different. I mean, something *really* different. It was the first time I'd ever talked to a journalist, and I figured they'd try to push us and try to make it sound like we were the bad guys. Little did I know they wanted to build a story around us, and not by turning us into either suspects or victims. Neville and I were detectives now. Not only that, but illustrious detectives. Neville told me to smile, be polite and only speak if necessary. He knew what he was doing, and I suspected that he had pulled some strings to get that interview.

When we jumped from the cab, there was a producer waiting, who led us into the building into an interviewing room. A reporter was already waiting for us. He was black and very tall, with a thin moustache and a shaved head. He shook Neville's hand like an old friend and didn't bother to say his name.

"Good morning, Sir Bartholomew," said the reporter. "Thanks for joining us. It's a pleasure to have you here. I imagine you are short of time."

"I always have time to talk to the press," said Neville. "How is Mrs West?"

"She's taking good care of the kids. And who is this?" asked Mr West, the reporter, pointing at me.

"This is Jerry," said Neville. "He's my assistant and apprentice. He's proving to be a very skilful investigator."

We sat by the table and West scribbled a few things in a notepad.

"What's your last name?" he asked me.

"Bellamy," Neville said. "Jerry Bellamy."

"Should I write 'assistant', 'apprentice' or 'detective'?" he asked after writing my name.

"Detective," I said, before Neville could answer. "I'm a detective."

Beside me, Neville shifted, and as I glanced at him I could tell he was getting annoyed that the attention had moved to me.

"Jerry has been of great help on some of my toughest cases," Neville broke in, smiling genially.

"I see," said West, turning the recorder on. "Well, I have to ask a few preliminary questions. There have been reports that London has a serial killer targeting actors. Can either of you comment on that?"

"I'm afraid I can't disclose information in an ongoing investigation," Neville said in his best Sherlock Holmes voice — as though it would sound like that on the printed page. "I can only say I fear these are dangerous times. For many, life no longer holds the value it once did. I have lost friends this week, very dear friends." He sighed dramatically as he saw he had the journalist's attention. "And it is my duty as an investigator and a human being to catch this killer."

I almost giggled. Within the same answer he had both refused to talk about the killer and admitted he was after him. And we were only getting started.

"Before we get going, I have to ask: how did you become a detective?" West asked.

Neville launched into his narrative, entirely in his element. "As I'm sure you're aware, I once played the character of Sherlock Holmes." We all knew that, but I guess he wanted to make sure West didn't forget it. "It was a wonderful job, but I had to abandon it due to social problems."

"What kind of social problems?" asked West, making a note on a pad. "Can you elaborate?"

"It was just...difficult for me to walk the streets of London, seeing so much crime, so much poverty, so much despair in the faces of people...my people." Neville's voice rang through the room, full of emotion. "I was paid a great deal of money to pretend to be someone else, and it wasn't fair to the people who watched every episode of my show. They were hungry, Mr. West. Hungry for justice. They saw me as a man who could solve any crime and bring balance to a world where good and evil aren't so distinguishable anymore."

Another dramatic pause. West didn't move.

"I was bringing the notion of justice to those people, and for a while that was good enough. But they needed something else, something higher. As an actor, I could promote that notion. But as a detective, I could bring justice to the streets. And that's how I became a private eye."

West flipped back a few pages in his notepad. "Yes, I see here that you've undergone the certification necessary for a private eye. Continue."

I felt compelled to explain that Neville had got that certification to play Sherlock Holmes, as any fan would know, but in the end I didn't say a word. He was having fun, and I decided not to interfere. Neville placed his hand on my shoulder and squeezed.

"When I found poor Mr. Bellamy here," he said, "he was nothing but a heroin fiend, a sick boy living in the worst kind of hole, surrounded by thugs and prostitutes."

This was news to me, and it took me a great deal of effort to keep my shock from showing on my face. West's eyes met mine and narrowed as he studied me.

"He was a crucial piece to solve the case I was investigating," Neville continued, "and thanks to him, that case was solved. So I decided to offer him a job and teach him how to strike back at the criminal world that had so devastated his life."

West looked at me like he was searching for confirmation.

"I did live in a hole," I said. An awkward silence followed.

West's attention went back to Neville. "How did you get involved in this particular case?"

Neville cleared his throat, a sorrowful look coming over his face.

"Since becoming a private eye," he said, "I have taken care not to lose contact with my fans. After all, *The Baker Street Sleuth* occupied some of the best years of my life. From time to time, I like to appear at conventions and get-togethers. Now, a few weeks ago, someone made contact with one of my former co-stars, Mr. Jay Mortigan. Professor Moriarty on the show, of course," he added.

"Yeah, I think I remember him," said West. "How's he involved, then?"

"Jay Mortigan and Lewis Thompson, one of my co-stars, had worked together on the stage. That's how he got the part."

"Lewis Thompson," said West, looking at his notes. "One of your recently deceased co-stars."

"Yes. Unfortunately, the actors who played the role of Dr Watson in the series have suffered an improbable number of accidents in recent weeks. Accidents," he added, "that I believe we both know were no such thing." He took a deep breath and then said, dramatically, "I have strong reasons to believe the murderer is Jay Mortigan."

West finished noting something down and then said, "I had a look at the copy of Thompson's memoir that you sent over. Where did you get it?"

I couldn't believe it: Neville had sent Thompson's memoir to the press? Who else had access to it? I almost asked it out loud, but once again preferred to keep my mouth shut.

"He was a dear friend," said Neville. "My investigation has revealed that one of the men who played the role of Watson possesses a secret that concerns Mr Mortigan. The thing is, he doesn't know which one of them it is. So he's been taking them out one by one, with the end result of possessing the secret himself while keeping it hidden from the rest of the world."

They kept talking. Neville kept spinning his bullshit, but I couldn't tell how much of it West bought. He didn't say much, just wrote down a lot and watched us both carefully.

183

There was no point to me being there; I sat and listened and, from time to time, agreed with whatever lie Neville had told that West wanted confirmed.

Finally, I asked to head out to the toilets; West offered to stop the interview until I returned, but both Neville and I said that that wasn't necessary, so at last I was able to escape. Once out of the office, I snuck my way out of the building.

It would have been nice to hop in a cab, but — story of my life — I had no money. Instead, I wandered up the street to the nearest red phone booth and rang Lucy. It wasn't until the call went dead that the fact that she wasn't there and couldn't answer really sunk in, and my eyes filled with tears.

CHAPTER THREE

Moriarty's Secretary

I ended up ringing Ace again; he sounded less than thrilled to hear my voice this time. The thrill of having being offered such a valuable piece of memorabilia was gone; now he was far more concerned about the rumours that were spreading.

"Somebody told me your house has been robbed," he said, and I couldn't tell if he was angry or just anxious. "And that a man came by to see you and found the whole place trashed. Rumour has it that this person was Sir Bartholomew Neville."

I felt compelled to deny it, but then decided to use it to my advantage. "So now you know," I said. "I'm working with the man. Where can we meet?"

"How did you met him, Bellamy?" he asked in an aggressive voice. "What trick did you use?"

I sighed. "Listen, Caesar, I'll tell you where I am. Come pick me up, and on the way to Mortigan's place I'll tell you everything you want to know."

Soon he appeared, driving a car so old and battered that I wasn't sure how it was still running. I slid into the passenger seat and closed my eyes.

"What the hell is going on?" he demanded, pulling away from the curb.

I reached for the magnifying glass in my jacket pocket. He stared at it for a long time, like he was afraid to touch it. Finally he picked it up and examined it.

"Guess you're pretty cosy with Neville these days, huh! How the hell did you end up his sidekick?"

I shrugged. "Your guess is as good as mine," I said. "We have somewhere to go, don't we?"

"Yeah, about that..." he said, and there was some joy in his voice. "I guess you had the wrong idea about it."

I looked at him, infuriated. "You're telling me you don't know where to find Mortigan?"

"Not completely," he said, putting the magnifying glass in his own jacket pocket. "You see, I did the whole interview by mail."

"By mail?!" I wanted to punch him in the face. "That's not what you wrote in the fanzine."

"I know, but it wouldn't sound good," he said. "But you see, I do have an address, I just don't know if he really lives there."

I must have had the most menacing expression on my face, because he was afraid to look me in the eyes. "You want to go there?" he asked in a low voice.

"We might as well," I said.

As Caesar drove me to that place, I told him a bunch of crap about how I'd made friends with Neville. On one hand, I didn't feel much like talking, but on the other one, it was a joy to torture him with those stories. We reached the address and Ace pulled over.

"We're here," he said, sounding annoyed.

"I'll go, then. It would be better if you didn't talk about this to anyone."

I was about to shut the door when he said, "Don't you think you could introduce me to Neville? After all, I am his biggest fan."

I thought about that for a second, and then scribbled a random address on a piece of paper, certainly not Neville's, and tucked it into Ace's breast pocket.

"He's not home right now," I said. "It would be best if you wait for this whole thing to blow over, you know, and then I can introduce you to him properly." I shrugged. "But if you can't wait, well, at least try to be polite when you meet him."

"Great," he said. "Oh, and also…"

"See you," I said, and shut the door with more strength than I needed to use.

It was yet another nice neighbourhood with dozens of old Victorian houses. The house I was looking for didn't stand out in any way, and it hardly looked like the lair of a criminal mastermind. Then again, Mortigan probably didn't actually live here.

I knocked on the door.

A middle-aged black woman opened it. "May I help you?"

"Hello, ma'am. Sorry to disturb you." I offered her a smile. "My name is Jerry Bellamy and I'm looking for Jay Mortigan. Is he in?"

She wasn't pleased to see me, I could tell. Mortigan's name had clearly rung a bell in her head, and the sound of that bell made her uncomfortable. "He's not in," she said at last.

"Ma'am," I said, showing her my Lestrade badge. "I'm a private detective, so if there's anything you can tell me about Mr. Mortigan…"

She hesitated. "Why don't you come in," she said. "And I'll tell you about Mr. Mortigan."

I followed her inside and sat at the kitchen table. I looked around; the place was nice. Clean. There were pictures on the wall of her and a man who wasn't Mortigan.

"My husband," she said, seeing that the pictures had caught my attention. "Gone these fifteen years, but I think of him every day." She handed me a cup of tea and added, "I'm Mildred, by the way. Mildred Hood. Hang on one second; I got to get something from the other room."

I sipped my tea. My gut told me that if Jay Mortigan had ever been here, it hadn't been for a long time — and I guessed he'd probably never been here at all.

She returned from the other room and plunked a box down on the table. "These are his," she said. "And his name wasn't Mortigan."

I looked up, genuinely surprised. "Really?"

"Yeah," she said.

I pulled the box close and peered inside. There were dozens of signed pictures of Mortigan dressed as Professor Moriarty. I had one of those myself in my flat.

She sat by my side as I looked through the box. The material was worth at least four thousand pounds. I was guessing that Mrs Hood probably didn't know that.

"Now, listen to me," she said. "This guy hired me a long time ago."

"Jay Mortigan, right?"

"That was his stage name," she agreed. "But his real name was Morton Price. He wanted an assistant, and I had experience working with actors. He came to me and said he was about to be a big name, that he was in some TV show and that sooner or later people would kill to have a signed photo." She looked down at her hands and sighed. "Thinking he was going to be this big shot, he decided to open an office and hire an agent. My job was to sit at a table and answer all the calls he thought he'd be getting from theatres and TV companies and films. He was sure the phone'd be ringing off the bloody hook. Problem was, nobody called, except for his mother, and you can't get very far when only your mum is interested in the work you do."

I nodded agreement.

"He was real chuffed, you know, real confident," she continued, "because he'd been told that the TV show was going to bring him back as Moriarty. They'd talked to his agent and to him and everything was looking promising. But a lot of things happened in the break, and it turned out when filming came around again that they'd decided to cut Moriarty for good. "

The fourth series, of course. When the new writers had gone mad. I wasn't surprised, really, that Moriarty had originally been in the cards to return. It was even less of a surprise that that idea had gone down the drain when the show picked back up again. Pretty much everything good about the show disappeared in series four.

"Mr Price stayed in his office all day," she said, "waiting and waiting for glory that never came. It was quite sad, you know, and rather pathetic. He was anticipating such a surge in popularity that he'd ordered dozens of photos, and with nothing else to do around the office he signed every last one of them. After a few months, it had become pretty obvious that no one was going to call, and he told me that he didn't have the money to pay me for my work. Since he didn't have anything else, he gave me a box of signed photos. Said they'd be worth a fortune one day." Shrugging, she added, "I sell a few, sometimes, but I've got a proper job now, so really all these photos are doing is gathering dust."

"Do you remember giving an interview in Mr Price's name?" I asked.

Mrs Hood stared at me with her eyes wide open. She put her cup of tea on the coffee table, trying not to shake too much, but still spilling some tea on her hand.

"Is that why you're here, detective?" she said. "I guess I'll tell you the truth: I gave a mail interview a couple of years ago. Someone sent me a letter after receiving one of Mr Price's signed photos. He wanted an interview with Mr Price. I thought it'd be a good chance to at least find more people to send photos to. Are you going to arrest me?" she asked, with fear in her voice, and then added, "Did I break the law somehow?"

I smiled at Mrs Hood, trying to seen friendly: "I'm not going to arrest you," I said. "But do you know where I can find Mr. Price?"

"I have no idea, I'm sorry," she said.

Well, that was a bummer, but then again it'd be silly to expect that Mortigan would be in that house just waiting for me.

"Have you heard from him since you stopped working for him?" I asked.

She shook her head. "Not that I'm surprised," she said. "I was never any more than a temp. I do hear about him, occasionally, though. Not Jay Mortigan, I mean, but Morton Price. Last time was, oh, two years ago? He was on TV, though I'm sorry to say it wasn't as an actor. He was on the news. He'd been arrested, though I can't quite remember anymore what for."

"Do you remember anything else?" I asked anxiously. "The location of the arrest? The news channel? The name of the reporter?"

"No. I'm sorry," she said. "I only saw it in passing, you know, and the only reason I noticed at all was because I recognised him."

This was all turning out to be really frustrating. I'd never been so close to finding out something important, only to discover that what I was looking for was still just out of reach.

"There is one other thing, though," Mrs Hood said suddenly. "Weird thing."

"Oh?"

"He mugged for the camera."

I was baffled. "What does that mean?"

"He made a funny face," she said. "Stretched his mouth and blinked repeatedly, like a crazy man."

Bill's words came back to my mind. "Like he was sending a message!" I said to myself. "Tell me, do you remember his mother's name? You said she used to ring up the office."

"It was Jane, I think. Yes, that was it, because there was a nurse who always used to make the call, and then once I answered she'd hand off the phone to Jane."

"A nurse? Was she in hospital?"

"No. She was in a care home, the poor dear."

"You by any chance remember which one?"

For once I was lucky.

CHAPTER FOUR

Crazy

Despite its name, Sunny Hills was a depressing little place, the kind of care home most people would avoid if they had any chance of getting in elsewhere. I walked in through the front doors and told the receptionist that I was an old family friend and that Mrs Price's son had asked me to look in on her. I was desperately hoping that she'd not passed away in the years that had gone by since Mrs Hood had last spoken to her.

Happily for me, she was still alive, though I figured she must be getting close to croaking. As the nurse walked with me to Mrs Price's room, she told me that Mrs Price would be celebrating her ninety-eighth birthday in two weeks.

"Does she have many visitors?" I asked.

"No," she said. "Her son used to come every week, but that stopped a couple of years back. Jane was devastated. She really loved him." She paused and opened a door. "Here we are."

Mrs Price was sitting on an old chair, a blanket over her knees and her hands folded on her lap. She was very small, lined and withered with age. Her face held great sadness, and she stared blankly at the floor. Sitting there, waiting for death to come.

"Jane!" said the nurse. "You have a visitor!"

Mrs Price slowly turned her head to look at us.

"Is it Mort?"

"I'm a friend of Mort's, Mrs Price," I said, coming into the room. "My name is John."

I sat in a chair in front of Mrs Price and took her hand in mine. Her skin was papery.

"I'll let you two have a nice chat," the nurse said. "I'll be right down the hall if you need me."

"Thanks," I said, and then turned my attention to Mrs Price. "Jane, I'm looking for Mort. Do you know where he is?"

"No," she said.

"Do you remember the last time you saw him?"

"Last time I saw Mort, he was crazy," she said.

"What do you mean?" I asked. "How was he crazy?"

"He kept saying all these crazy things," she said. Her voice was wispy. "He was never the same after what happened, you know?"

"After what happened?" I asked. She'd gone quiet, staring across the room, so I tried again. "I need to find Mort, Mrs Price. Your son. It's very important. Do you know where he is?"

"He used to come here every week with presents," she said. "He'd sit and listen and sit and listen…"

"That's very nice of him," I said, thinking to myself that he must have ended up bored to tears.

"He was a good boy," she said. "A good son." Her mind clearly drifted for a moment, but then she said, "Then he didn't listen so good anymore."

"What do you mean?"

"He starts coming in and rattling away," she said. "Crazy stuff. Came to me because I was the only one who'd listen to him...because I'm his mother."

"What did he say?" I was getting impatient, but I could tell that there wasn't any point to trying to hurry Mrs Price along. She was old, and I guessed probably somewhere on the road to senile, and as much as I wanted to know everything she did immediately, it seemed I was going to have to wait.

"Crazy stuff," she repeated. "Said he was going to be rich and powerful. Said he was on his way to being the greatest criminal mastermind London had ever seen. Said he'd got it all planned out and that no one could stop him." She suddenly looked terribly small and terribly vulnerable. "Sometimes he scared me," she whispered. "Got this look in his eyes."

"Did he say anything else?" I asked.

She thought about that for a minute. "He said he was going to make a lot of money," she said at last. "Said he was going to buy a large house and take me there, so I could be with him the rest of my life."

"Did you tell anyone about this?"

"Said something to the nurse," she said. "She told me not to worry, that I was imagining things. I'm old and my mind doesn't always work all that well, you know, so no one takes me seriously."

"I take you seriously," I said. "Do you have any idea where Mort might be now?"

"Could be anywhere," she said impatiently. "Told you, he's crazy. Could be anywhere, doing anything."

"Look, Mrs Price," I said. "I really need to know…"

She was starting to get agitated. "Are you going to bring Mort back?" she asked, and pressed a button by the side of the bed. She was calling the nurse. There were still a lot of questions I had to ask her, but I couldn't do it with the nurse by our side. So I got up and showed myself the way out. Maybe I'd come back another day, bringing flowers and chocolates. But for now all I had was another dead end.

I'd never have guessed that finding Mortigan would be so much harder than finding Neville. And now I was stuck, with nowhere to go and no idea of where to look next. Mortigan's mother had been my last idea.

Her words rang in my mind as I walked down the street. 'He's gone crazy'. I wondered if the desire for power could have turned him into a lunatic — could he possibly believe he was actually Moriarty? Could he be that delusional?

I wished I'd been able to get more information out of Mrs Price. I'd no doubt she knew more than she was saying, but it was possible that the information locked in her head might never be accessed. It was too bad, because I was sure that somewhere in that head of hers was something that would have led me to Mortigan.

The worst bit was feeling so helpless, knowing that while I kept hitting dead ends that Lucy might be suffering at Mortigan's hands.

I was deep in thought when a hand grabbed my shoulder. I panicked and a voice told me to be calm. I turned my head to find Scorsese, whose smile was missing today.

"Get in the car," he said.

The black sedan must have been out of commission, because my ride for the day was a silver minivan. Bill wasn't there, but there was a small TV, broadcasting the finding of the body of David Elroy, the final Watson on our list.

CHAPTER FOUR

The Eyewitness

There were already a few reporters when I got to Elroy's house. They ran in my direction, pointing their microphones at me. I ran into a bobby and told him I was a friend of the victim's, so he helped me enter the house, into the crime scene, where the press couldn't bother me.

"This is crazy!" said the bobby as he shut the door behind me. "We get calls for this kind of thing every day, but this is the first time I've seen so many of these jackals in one place."

"Was Elroy murdered?" I asked him.

"Yeah," he said. "It's a pretty gruesome crime scene; hope you've got a strong stomach."

"I'm Private Detective Bellamy," I said, showing him my Lestrade badge. He was so agitated he barely looked at it. "Is Sir Bartholomew Neville inside?"

"Yeah, he keeps asking for you."

"Catch me up," I said.

"Two dead bodies," he said, leading the way through the house. "One male, the other female. The man is David Elroy, the occupant of the house. He was killed in the kitchen; looks like he was making breakfast and didn't hear the killer enter over the noise of the blender. Shot three times in the back. ME says it looks like the first bullet went straight in through the back of the head and exited through the forehead and, pending an autopsy, that's the likely cause of death. The other two were just insurance. He was dead before hitting the floor."

"What about the female?" I had to ask, but I had a bad feeling I already knew the answer.

"Red-haired girl in her twenties," he said. "No ID yet, but it looks like a murder-suicide; looks like she popped him and then killed herself."

I swallowed. It's funny; on TV, the hero usually manages to keep his composure when someone close to them dies. But I wasn't a hero. I'd known it was coming, really; Lucy had been in Mortigan's hands for a long time. She'd been dead from the moment he caught her. And it was my fault. I'd been the one who wanted to go back to the motel, and now she was dead.

"Her name was Lucy," I said faintly.

"You okay, mate?" the bobby said. "You know the girl?"

"Something like that," I said, feeling weak.

"You sure you're okay to go in and see the bodies? If you're going to be sick or faint or something you should probably stay out here."

"No, I'll be fine," I said. "Just…give me a minute."

He shrugged. "Suit yourself." He handed me a pair of disposable booties. "Just put these on when you come into the crime scene, okay? Don't want you tracking anything in or out."

He disappeared through the kitchen door, leaving me alone, and the tears began to trickle down my cheeks. It took me a couple of minutes to get control over my emotions and dry off my face. The last thing I wanted was to cry in front of everyone.

I took a deep breath. From the moment I went through that door, I was an actor playing a tough detective, and tough detectives don't cry.

I entered the kitchen. The place was hell. David Elroy was face down on the floor, the back of his head a bloody mess. Blood and brain matter splattered the counter and cabinets in front of him, and a congealing pool of blood mixed with the spilled smoothie on the floor. The blender cup had fallen from his hand as he'd gone down and lay on its side, the pink liquid creating a barrier against which the blood built up. It was pretty obvious he'd been taken by surprise, and no wonder. The noise of the blender would have been enough to drown out almost anything else, including the sound of footsteps behind him.

I turned around, following the line of the bullets' trajectory, and found Lucy in a corner. The gun that had murdered Elroy had fallen by her side; she'd fired three times, so assuming the gun had been fully loaded, there were five bullets left unused. She hadn't used the gun to kill herself; a bottle of bleach had tipped on its side, the spilt liquid staining her clothes. Her pretty face was blue and frozen in an expression of horror that I knew would haunt my nightmares for years. Foam bubbled over her lips and down her chin. Her right eye bore the imprint of a bruise that was three or four shades darker than the rest of her face.

The Scene of Crime Officers (SOCOs) were going over the kitchen with a fine-toothed comb. Every few seconds I heard the click of a camera as someone recorded a pertinent piece of evidence. I hovered at the edge of the kitchen, unsure of what to do. It was a little surreal that I was allowed to be there, that no one was kicking me out. I didn't belong there. I felt like an intruder, who just wanders around trying to be invisible. But I wouldn't be invisible forever, that's for sure. I tried to blend in for a while, not to comment or anything, but after a few minutes I decided I needed to at least try to do something, to try to make a difference.

Staying out of the SOCOs way, I walked around the kitchen, trying to take in as much as possible without touching anything. There had to be something on the floor, on the walls, on the bodies — no one could come in contact with something else without leaving something of themselves behind.

I didn't want to look at Lucy's face again, but it was necessary. I had to do my job. I stared at her for a long time, until I began to feel, quite clearly, that her body was trying to tell me something. It was there, I knew it, but I couldn't figure out what it was. Was it her expression? Her eyes?

"She certainly did it."

I turned my head. Neville had just entered the kitchen and was staring at me with a displeased expression.

"Hello, Jerry," he said peevishly. "I didn't appreciate you vanishing earlier."

"Sorry," I said untruthfully.

"Hmm," he said. "Have I told you my theory?"

"What theory?"

"Apparently not." He looked around the kitchen, shaking his head sadly, and then said, "Your pretty redhead was working for Mortigan. She was a trained assassin, playing the jigsaw crockery routine to get away with the murder of Lewis Thompson. It would probably have worked if you and I hadn't entered the case. The girl realised she was going to get caught, but she was afraid of her employer more than she was afraid of the two of us. Knowing she was probably going to die, she finished her job and tried to tie up all the loose ends that could lead back to Mortigan. And that left one final problem to resolve: her. So in order to finally finish the job, she offered herself." He looked sorrowfully down at her body. "We just aren't sure why she opted to poison herself instead of putting a bullet through her brain."

He said all that casually, like he was talking about a soccer game or a cake recipe. At that moment I wished I could kill him. Everything he said made perfect sense, and I hated that it did. I wanted to strangle him. But I knew I'd need my energy later, because when I found Mortigan, I planned to kill him slowly.

It was kind of hard to justify my fury, though, because the more I thought about it, the more it seemed likely that the Lucy I'd fallen in love with wasn't a real person.

"The cops agree with my assessment of the whole situation," Neville said nonchalantly. "There are no signs of a struggle on either victim, which means the girl must have walked into the kitchen of her own free will. No one forced her, at least not physically. The GST test confirms she did fire the gun herself. She didn't take any forensic countermeasures; she walked in expecting to die. It's too soon for us to draw any conclusions about that.

We're sure to know more once the SOCOs have finished collecting and analysing the evidence.

"Shut up," I said, massaging my temples. "Let me think."

What was I looking for? He'd drawn me a perfect picture. Lucy's kidnapping? Staged. The tall man? A hired hitman. The reason for the entire thing? God knew. Mortigan could have had a million reasons.

As far as we knew, Lucy's father hadn't even been a Watson. I struggled to think clearly. Was there any proof that Lucy herself wasn't a hired agent?

"We got to get out there," said Neville. "These people are dying for an interview."

"You go if you want," I said. "I'm busy in here."

'Look at everything again!' I told myself.

A kitchen. A sink, a tap, a blender, a cupboard, lots of knives, spoons and forks. Protein shake, flour, sugar, salt. A porcelain cow dressed as a chef. Pretty standard kitchen.

A dead man on the floor, his blood creeping away from what was left of his head.

And Lucy.

Her black eye.

Without even thinking, I knelt next to Lucy and rubbed at her right eye, the one with the bruise.

"Oi, mate, get off!" a cop shouted. Hands grabbed me and pulled me away from Lucy's body, and I was escorted out of the kitchen, a bobby left to keep an eye on me.

It didn't matter, though. I stared at my finger, mesmerised by the small, dark purple splotch. It was makeup.

"Jesus, Jerry!" Neville snapped. "Get hold of yourself, boy. Keep acting like this and they'll boot both of us off this investigation!"

But I was laughing. If this was a joke, I was starting to get it. God Almighty in heaven, and Jesus and all the saints, I was starting to get it!

CHAPTER FIVE

Dead People

As the hunt for Jay Mortigan continued, Neville and I continued to accrue more and more fame. West's article had sold a lot of magazines, and after it was followed by Lucy's death, we became the talk of the town. I didn't want it, but a Sherlock needs his Watson, and Neville had fastened onto me. I probably should have a bit cross for being exposed, but in a way it was kind of distracting. It kept the anger, sadness, grief and fear from bubbling over and exploding.

It also didn't hurt that my talk show appearances and the photos with Neville had started to generate some very welcome income for me, which was useful, since I had no real job anymore. But the best part of it was when Caesar Ace asked me for an interview for his fanzine. I almost said yes just to mess a little bit more with him, but in the end decided not to answer his calls. It wasn't so much fun after Lucy was gone.

The really weird thing was that I was suddenly surrounded by admirers. I had never been in the spotlight before, and was used to be either ignored or laughed at. But now I suddenly was an important person. Okay, not as important as Neville, he was the real star, but I was getting a lot of attention too. People I knew started to call and ask for favours. People I didn't know wanted to take a picture with me. Even Pete called, inviting me for dinner at his place. He said he was sorry for not believing me before and that baby Norman was excited about having a famous uncle.

"Come for Sunday roast," he said. "We'll invite some family friends, for old time's sake."

It was the greatest opportunity I could ever have to either get close to my brother again or snub him. After all those years of being in his shadow, I was finally the one who'd done something right.

It was tempting to tell him that my schedule was full but that if he rang back in a week I could try to fit him in, but Pete didn't really deserve that. He wasn't a bad person, he was just...normal. And normal people weren't my kind of people. So I just said I didn't think it was a good idea. I didn't like the idea of being flattered by people who usually despised me — which, to a certain extent, included everyone in my family.

I moved in at a small lodge. Neville paid for my lodging as part of my commission. It was nice while it lasted, at least; I didn't dare to ask who was signing the cheques. I had food, clothes, transportation — if someone had asked me if I wanted to take another case, the answer would have been simple. Why bother? This one paid all the bills. They even got me a legit detective certificate, and I didn't dare to ask where they got it from, either.

The Watson Murders were rapidly becoming one of the most popular cases in the history of the UK. My role was a supporting one. Our agent suggested I grow a moustache, so I did. Someone else said I should present myself as Dr Bellamy, but that was too much. It took the illusion too far — no one was going to believe I was a doctor, and anyway anyone who spent two minutes checking me out would pretty easily figure out that that was a lie. Anyway, nobody expected me to make wise remarks, or even to talk at all. All I had to do was to emphasise what a genius Neville was, and that wasn't a difficult task. He was a showman. He had charisma, intelligence and wit, and he was a good enough actor to make it seem like all of those things were phenomenal.

Scotland Yard was doing everything in their power to locate Mortigan, but it was proving to be an impossible task. Neville used this. In every interview he made it seem like he had a really good lead on Mortigan, strongly hinting that his chances of finding the man were much higher than the police's chances.

That, of course, was ridiculous. I was actually ahead of them all! I knew Mortigan's real name, something no one else had been able to track down. If the police had had that information, they could have found him in the blink of an eye. But I didn't want that to happen. I wanted to find Mortigan myself. I had no intention of bringing him in. I had bigger plans for Jay Mortigan.

Nobody had come to the morgue to identify Lucy's body, and I didn't want her to be buried as a Jane Doe. I went and identified her, using the name she had given me the first night we met. Now that I had a little money, I was able to ensure that she got a decent funeral. It was a simple graveside service, and I had them open the casket before lowering it into the ground. The mortician had done a wonderful job; the horrible blue cast to Lucy's skin was gone, and she looked peaceful. She was beautiful, with the face of an angel. There were no scars, no marks and no black eye. She was perfect.

The day was bright and sunny, which made things somehow sadder, and as I walked through the cemetery, Bill fell in step beside me.

"I'm sorry," he said.

I almost didn't recognise him; I'd never seen him out of the suit, and the Hawaiian shirt and khakis were completely unexpected.

"Don't be," I said.

"We need to talk."

"Yes, I know," I said. "I've been doing a lot of thinking, you know. There's something behind all this. Some real conspiracy. And I don't know if I want to talk to you about it. I don't know which side to take."

He thrust his hands in his pockets and looked up at the cloudless sky. "Take the right side, of course."

"I don't know which one that is." I sighed. "Have you talked to the motel clerk?"

"We're working on that."

"I thought you might be." I stopped and turned to him. "You know, I think you've made some mistakes."

"What do you mean?"

"You explained how the information war worked, remember? I don't think you should have done that. For your own sake, I mean. Not mine."

"What are you talking about?"

I sat on a nearby gravestone and took my jacket off.

"It's not completely clear in my mind yet. I think... I think some of it is real. The war? Maybe. Your story, that whole man in black charade? I think that's just part of the joke. A very important part. You work for someone, that's for sure. I just don't know who."

He sat by my side and sighed.

"I wish you weren't so smart," he said. "I wish we'd met under different occasions. I like you, Jerry, but I don't like this. This whole thing, it's just a mess."

I agreed. "It's a big game planned by someone who's not that good at planning games." I glanced sideways at him. "You know who's doing all this, don't you?"

He pulled a pack of gum from his pocket, put a piece in his mouth and chewed it in silence for a moment.

"Yes," he said at last. "I know who's doing all this. It's someone I don't respect." He hesitated. "I would love to see you orchestrating something like this, my friend. It would be beautiful. You, I respect."

"You're not going to tell me who it is, are you?"

"You're close. I think you've already figured it out," he said, and then added, "I believe you have the right to figure it out by yourself. I could just spill it out to you right now, but it doesn't seem right. I believe you're close to the truth by now."

"I have a good theory," I answered.

"What's keeping you from taking action, then?" he asked.

"I have to find something out," I said.

He sighed, seeming a bit disappointed. "I saw you on TV," he said, but I didn't think that was what was on his mind.

"I thought you didn't watch TV."

He laughed. "I love television!" He removed his gum from his mouth, stuck it under the gravestone and then stood up and looked down at me. "We'll probably never meet again. I got to head out of town for a year or two. But I'm guessing you'll be on TV.

"I guess."

"Do me a favour?" he said. "When you go, remove that piece of gum I just stuck in there. It wasn't a nice thing for me to do."

"Yeah, okay," I said.

He turned to go, and then said, "My name actually is Bill, by the way. Thought you might like to know."

"It's been a pleasure," I said.

He went downhill to the cemetery gates and went away. As soon as he was gone, I detached the piece of gum; there was a piece of paper with the name 'Alfred Adler' on it.

Less than an hour later I was at Sunny Hills, where I learned that Mrs Price had passed away that morning. My paranoid mind immediately created all sorts of scenarios in which the old lady had been murdered. The nurses said Mortigan hadn't visited her since I'd been to see her, but I knew there were a million ways he could arranged for her death without having to show up. I decided to pay for her funeral expenses as well. I think somebody somewhere would've appreciated the gesture.

CHAPTER SIX

No Business Like the Murder Business

Sandra Thompson was a small, good-looking American who liked to wear lemon green dresses and huge pearl necklaces that made her look like a Flintstones reject. She was Neville's and my agent. She took us around, made appointments and gave us instructions about how to act in front of the camera. Her instructions weren't always pleasant to follow, but she knew what she was doing. We were getting some money from TV appearances, and I was starting to think of becoming a professional detective, now that I at least had a certificate. I wasn't an actor and couldn't survive on fame for the rest of my life. Neville loved every minute of the farce. The police had determined that Lucy was the killer, and with her death, the case was officially closed. But Sandra was marketing Mortigan as the big villain behind it all. That meant we technically still had a killer to catch, a killer that the police weren't bothered about catching because there wasn't any evidence.

But even then Neville was too busy to do any actual investigative work. We jumped from one interview to the next without pausing for breath. And there was a rumour going around that he was about to sign for a revival of *The Baker Street Sleuth*.

"You have to take care of your personal image, Jerry," Sandra said as the makeup artist worked on my face. "Don't forget that's what you're selling here."

"I was never much of a salesman, Sandy," I said, staring at my reflection. "You should have seen me at work. I could barely bag eggs without breaking them."

"You've come up in the world," she said. "In ten minutes you'll be on national TV, and it's your job to look good."

"My job is to make Neville look good," I answered. "And that's not even a real job."

"Stop complaining," she said. "Remember your life before this whole thing? Do you want to go back to that?"

No, I didn't. It was weird to picture myself going back to that tiny house, kept company only by memorabilia, with nothing more exciting that being chewed out every night at Goodwill Quick Market. Life was better now, in a million different ways. But something had been lost along the way. I couldn't really tell what it was; just that it wasn't there anymore.

"Look at him," she said and pointed at Neville. "Makeup is a formality for that man. He belongs to the cameras. But he's included you in this whole thing, so don't embarrass us. You're not handsome or charismatic, but there's no accounting for taste." She frowned at me. "This isn't your world, Jerry. In a couple of days we're going to be signing contracts, but everything depends on tonight. You only have yourself to think of, but some of us have families. So be good tonight."

"I'll do my best," I said. "It's just that this is all kinda new to me."

"Just be pleasant and say what everyone wants to hear."

Nobody could blame me for being uneasy, but in reality I was just bored. After living my whole life in front of the TV, I was finally on the other side of the camera, and suddenly all I wanted was to go back to the real world. There was a real world out there, right? A world where real people had real problems and had to find real solutions for them? I was suddenly overcome with the desire to give that world a chance.

The host presented us to the public, and we both smiled at the camera. All I had to say was 'it's a pleasure to be here'; after that, I could have exploded and nobody would have noticed it. I could hardly remember the name of the woman who was talking to us, or even the name of the show.

The host had perfectly white teeth and an insincere smile. Turning that smile on Neville, she said, "Everyone's been following your investigation in the last couple of weeks. It all started at a convention, is that right?"

Neville gave her a friendly smile. "Yes. I was speaking to the fans of my show when a young woman asked me about her father's murder."

"Now, is this the young woman recently involved in the murder of David Elroy?"

"That's right," said Neville. "I'm afraid the poor dear committed suicide after shooting Elroy. Rather shockingly, after putting all of the pieces together, we've begun to realise that this girl was part of a bigger conspiracy to frame me for those murders, if you can believe it."

"But why did she kill herself?" the host asked.

"We believe she was feeling guilty for her actions," said Neville. "She wasn't the mastermind behind the murders, but she certainly had a hand in them."

"Now, we've heard rumours that Jay Mortigan, who played Professor Moriarty on your show, may in fact be the mastermind behind everything," said the host, and then added, "That he was this young woman's boss! What can you tell us about this?"

"Some people can't tell the difference between fiction and reality," he said sadly. "Jay Mortigan was a very strange man, obsessed with his role."

"Do you mean he was a method actor?" the host asked.

"Not at all, my dear! Method acting is a noble art that has is practiced by many fine actors, including myself. What we are dealing with here is pure insanity."

I couldn't help but giggle. And suddenly everyone was looking at me.

"Mr. Bellamy," the host said pleasantly. "Would you like to weigh in on this? What is it about this case that you find so humorous?"

I looked at Neville. His face was relaxed, but a small drop of sweat on his forehead told me to fix things really quickly, or the situation was going to get ugly for both of us. He wanted to sign those contracts, for commercials and books and movies and new episodes of his TV series. My ill-timed giggle could put all that in jeopardy.

My eyes went to the crowd watching us. They were just a tiny fraction of the country sitting in front of their TVs. They seemed curious and nervous. And poor Sandra! She must be grabbing her blonde hair backstage, wondering why she let me take part in the interview in the first place. Once again, I was the number that didn't fit in the equation. As I had been all my life.

"Yes, actually," I said, looking directly at the camera. "There is something funny. You know, I grew up watching Sir Bartholomew as Sherlock Holmes. I knew the names and faces of every single one of the actors who have died at Mortigan's hands. Today, we are here to warn England that Mortigan is still out there, and he is dangerous." I took a deep breath. "For Mortigan, fiction has become reality. He has become the character he played — or so it seems. How can a fictional character exist in the real world? How can he eat, drink, sleep and continue doing every tiny thing a human being does, and yet continue to be that character?" I was speaking quite rapidly now. I didn't care there were thousands of people listening to me; it was like I was speaking to myself in the mirror, trying to make sense out of everything that'd happened. "I'm sorry for my inappropriate laughter," I said, "but I just find it funny that we seem to be looking for Moriarty, when really what we're looking for is a man who's delusional. If he's gone crazy…and if he's still out there…should we be looking for the evil mastermind of Moriarty or for someone less…or maybe someone more dangerous? And the only way I can…"

They were all looking at me. They wanted me to conclude that line. But I couldn't. It was too much for me. I just stared at the floor and sighed. Neville took it from there:

"I think what Jerry is trying to say is that he and we can't pretend to be Holmes and Watson," he said. "We are not. We are two flesh and blood people, but that doesn't mean we are going to let this vicious murderer escape from justice. You have my word on that."

They applauded him. I was still staring at the floor. I wanted to finish that sentence, but would never be able to do it, at least not with words. The show was his for the rest of the night. Those contracts would be signed after all.

Not with words…

CHAPTER SEVEN

The Penultimate Problem

"That wasn't too bad," Sandra told me as the cab pulled up to my lodge. "A bit melodramatic, but I think you nailed it."

"Thanks, Sandra," I said, with a sad smile.

"But next time let me know what you're going to say," she said. "A wrong sentence can doom everything we're trying to build in here."

I just nodded. I wasn't listening to her; I was trying to remember everything I'd said. I was just thinking out loud back then, but there was something very important in my words — but I just couldn't figure out what it was.

"You could do great things," said Sandra, and she sounded sincere.

"Yeah, right," I said.

"I mean it," she said, sounding somewhat motherly. "That was a nice speech. You should be proud."

"Should I?" I asked, avoiding her eyes. "It all smells like bullshit to me."

"Get a good night's sleep," she said. "We have a long day tomorrow."

I shut the cab door and went into the lodge. The stairways were empty, and so was the hallway. I was ready to throw myself in bed and sleep all night, hoping to dream of somewhere else. But when I turned the light on, the room remained dark.

A man's voice in the corner told me to chill.

"If you scream," he said, "I'll have to put a bullet in your chest, and that wouldn't be good for either of us. I want to talk to you, and trust me, we have quite a lot to discuss. So please, sit down."

I stayed cool. Somehow, I had expected that visit. Whatever the man in the dark had to say, I wanted to hear. So I sat on the couch and stared at the corner.

"So, you're Mort?" I asked, squinting my eyes trying to see him better.

"I'm death," he said. His voice sounded a bit familiar, but I couldn't figure out where I had heard it before. "But that doesn't matter. Somebody you know very well has double-crossed me. Do you know who I'm talking about?"

"I'm not sure," I said. "And I don't know how you fit in all this."

"I thought you were smarter," he said, lighting a cigarette. "I'm not the one you call Mort. And what about you? Should I call you Watson Number Six?"

"What do you want?" I asked, a bit annoyed.

"I told you. Someone double-crossed me," said the man in the dark. "He promised me something — he promised us all something — and now he doesn't want to pay me. He brought Lucy to a gruesome end, and if he'd had his way he'd have had me go the same way. But I'm not that easy to deceive."

"So this is about revenge?" I asked, very confused.

"Revenge is a poor plot device, Watson Number Six," he said. "This is more about curiosity, really. After all, there's got to be something big behind all this. Money? Power? Whatever it is, I wouldn't mind getting a share. I've been watching you from a distance. At first, I thought you were just another one of his pals. Now I see there's something bigger and meaner in his game. You know quite a bit of what's going on, but you don't know enough."

"You're the tall man," I said, and there was no doubt in my voice. "You're a hitman."

"I never liked that word," he said.

"Did you kill Lucy?" I asked.

"If she didn't follow her instructions, then my job was pull the trigger, you know?"

"So if she didn't kill Elroy and then commit suicide, you were going to blow her brains out. She didn't have a choice. You might as well have killed her."

He laughed loudly, like I had just told him the greatest joke in the world. But my eyes were starting to grow accustomed to the dark. He had a pistol in his gloved hands, blue garbage bags around his feet and a rubber cap on his head. I just couldn't see his goddamn face.

"She was never the target," he said. "The gun was pointed at you."

"At me?" I was shocked. "So you mean that..."

I couldn't finish the thought, but it was all pretty obvious now. Lucy had had orders to murder the fifth Watson and then kill herself, making it look like she was working for Mortigan. No, it was more than that: making it look like she wanted it to look like a double homicide. Make people think they're smart, make they think they're ten steps ahead of you. They made us think she was a suicidal fanatic, when in reality she was coerced to be part of the carnage. If she hadn't pulled the trigger, the tall man would have killed me. Lucy had chosen death rather than let me die. That meant she really had cared for me.

"The orders were for her to put a bullet in her brain," the man in the dark said. "Lord knows why she drank the bleach instead."

"She wanted to preserve her face," I said.

"Why?"

"I think I'm the only person in the world who knows the answer to that question."

"I don't need your answers," he said. "If the dead bitch wanted to send you some message, that isn't my business. All I want is to be face to face with Sir Bartholomew Neville."

"He won't be here tonight, if that's what you're hoping for," I said. That conversation was getting to a critical point. I had to get ready for action. "I think he's busy posing for some beer advertisement."

"That goddamn piece of shit!" he shouted. "I'm sorry, how did a smart guy like you get involved with that scumbag?"

"I was a fan of his show," I said. "Past tense. Are we going to work together, or will next time be like this again: a dark room and one of us pointing a gun at the other?"

"I think the best thing would be killing you and then killing him. There are a whole lot of mysteries around, but I'm not a detective. I'm just a freelancer. Although I am a bit curious to see the end of this story."

The sound of the gun trigger spoke for him. There was a heavy metal statuette close enough to where I was sitting. All I had to do was to grab it and break his arm before he hit me. After that, I could hold him until the police arrived. But I had to buy some time, just until my eyes got more used to the dark.

"How do you plan to get to Neville?" I asked, trying not to sound too nervous.

"I haven't planned that yet," he said. "The guy is everywhere, nowadays. I'll think of something."

"And after that?" I said, with my eyes on the statuette. "Do you think you can kill one of the most beloved men in England and just walk away?"

"Yes. Pretty much."

'Maybe it would be better for both of us if you don't shoot me."

"Why?"

"I have a message from your mother."

"A message from my…?"

It was my chance. I grabbed the statuette from the side table and threw it at his face. I heard the wet sound of his face being bashed in. He fell back, almost letting the gun fall, and I jumped into the darkness. He got off a few shots, but he was dazed and it was dark, and the bullets went wide. He couldn't see me running in the shadows, but I could see his silhouette against the window. He ran out of bullets, and I ran in his direction and hit him with the statuette several times in the back. The room was pitch black and I couldn't see him, but I could hear the sound of his bones breaking as I struck him repeatedly.

When he finally stopped moving, I dropped the statuette, got up and turned the table lamp on. I knew the man on the floor. He wasn't smiling and wasn't wearing a suit, but there was no way of denying it: that was definitely the Scorsese fellow who used to accompany Bill. It took me a little longer to realise that he was dead.

I knew I had to call the police immediately, but instead I went for his pockets. He had a keychain, a parking ticket and a black leather wallet with some money in it. His documents said that his name was Martin Woodward, 34 years old. He also had a certificate from the Actors Guild of Great Britain that proved he was a professional actor.

CHAPTER EIGHT

Epiphany

The phone rang five times before Pete picked it up. I don't know how I must have sounded, calling him at two AM, but he sounded genuinely concerned when he heard my voice.

"Where are you, Jerry?" he asked.

"I'm at the police station," I said. "I…I just killed a man."

He fell silent for a moment, and then almost shouted: "You did what?"

I could hear Kara asking him what happened. They had probably already been sleeping when I called. "Don't worry," I said. "It was self-defence. I'll have to answer a lot of questions tonight, but I don't think I'll get arrested."

"Oh, my god!" he said. "Are you alright?"

"I'm fine," I said. "Got a few bruises, but nothing serious. They said I could make a call, and I didn't know who else I could…"

"Please, just give me a second," he said. I could hear Pete arguing with Kara. A few seconds later he came back. "I'll answer you from my office."

I had to wait half a minute until he picked the phone up again and said, "Okay, just tell me everything from the start."

I tried to sum up what had happened. I had already told that story five times that night, and would probably spend the rest of the night telling it again. Pete just kept quiet and listened while I told him my fight with Scorsese.

"And then I called the cops myself," I said. "They saw his gun on the floor and that he broke in, so I guess I won't have much trouble in making my defence."

"And do you want me to get you a lawyer?" Pete asked. "I know some people who can help you. Just let me make a few calls…"

"I didn't call you for that, Pete," I said. "I called you because everyone I care about is either dead or gone, and I only have you in the world."

He fell silent again. I'd never spoken like that to him before. He cleared his throat and then said: "You want me to meet you there?"

"Yes," I said, sobbing. "Yes, I would."

I gave Pete the police station address and waited for him in a hallway with a cup of coffee in my hand. He got there in half an hour. His hair was messed and his pants didn't match his shoes, something that in normal circumstances would be unthinkable for him.

"Hey there," he said, sitting by my side.

"Sorry to call you at this hour," I said. "How are things at home?"

"I had a fight with Kara," he said, frowning.

"What did you tell her?" I asked.

"The minimum," he said. "That you were in trouble. That you needed me. She was infuriated, and shouted so hard she woke Norman up."

I gave a sad smile. "I'm sorry to drag you into this," I said. "Good news is I think I'll be able to go home before midnight. Bad news is I have nowhere to go."

"You need money for a hotel?" he asked.

"I have places I can stay," I said. "I think you didn't understand what I meant."

Pete sighed. "What about that friend of yours? That actor?"

I drank the rest of my coffee and crunched the disposable plastic cup. "I really don't want to think about him right now."

"So what now?" Pete asked. "You're not asking me to take you home."

"I wouldn't dream," I said. "Don't want to ruin your perfect life."

"Please, don't start again," he said.

"I'm serious this time, Pete," I said. "I don't want to ruin your life. I've ruined too many lives already. I do that to people. It's the only thing I do well."

I was crying already. Pete hugged me, and I dripped a river of tears in his shoulder. "Easy there, mate," he said. "You got to be strong."

"I'm not strong," I said. "I'm just a worthless piece of shit. I can't do nothing right, and for a while that only meant messing my life up. But now people are dying and I don't know what else to do."

I cried there for a long time, until somebody called me for interrogation. "I have to go now," I said to Pete. "Please, go back home. Pretend this didn't happen."

"I'll wait for you," he said.

"No, you won't," I replied.

I got up and followed the officer to the DI's office. He was a forty-year-old man with grey hair and a black moustache. He was examining a file as I entered. "Take a seat, Mr Bellamy," he said, and so I did. "We have some news for you. It seems that the man who attacked you indeed was Martin Woodward, and as far as we know, he was no hitman. That's good for you, since a hitman would've probably just shot you point blank without giving you the chance to fight back."

He licked his finger and turned a page on his file. "He was an actor, though we discovered he hadn't got much work lately. He hadn't been in a play for a couple of years, and before that he was an extra on TV." He raised his eyes from the file and stared at me. "Are you following?"

"Yes," I said.

"Good," he said, "because having watched you on TV a few times and knowing your past, the next part is going to sound a little strange. Mr Woodward worked as an extra in a TV show named *The Baker Street Sleuth.*"

Somehow, I wasn't very surprised. It didn't sound that strange, though I wasn't really sure why. It wasn't the missing piece of the puzzle that I was looking for. There was still something else, something hidden in that whole case, and I couldn't figure out what it was.

"Have you ever seen Mr. Woodward before?" he asked.

"No," I answered.

"You do have a friend who starred in that same show, don't you?"

"He's not my friend," I said. "He's my partner."

"The question is the same," the DI said. "Did you know him?"

I answered without hesitation: "No. I had never seen him before tonight."

He stared at me, like he didn't believe what I was saying. "Okay, I won't hold you for much longer," he said. "Since your testimony seems legit, everything indicates that he was attacking you and that you only defended yourself. I will need you to come back, though. This all still seems very odd."

Pete was waiting for me as I walked out the room. "I told you not to wait for me," I said.

"We need to talk," he said.

"I don't want to hear a sermon right now, Pete."

"I mean a normal talk," he said. "You need to talk to someone, I can see that."

"Okay, then," I said. "Let's go to a pub."

We drank a couple of pints and talked about our childhood and how things were much easier then. I felt he really was listening, so I said everything I had on my mind. It had been so long since I had had a proper chat with someone who was listening that I just spilled it all out to him. Pete was surprised to hear all the little details of my adventures, and I didn't know if he did believe it all. But it was good to be able to tell him all that. I even told him about Lucy, about her death and how I truly missed her.

"It was an odd affair, and I'm aware of that," I said. "But I can't remember ever being in a normal, healthy relationship."

"Maybe you're looking in the wrong places," Pete said, looking at me, concerned. "There are good women out there, Jerry."

"Like Kara?" I asked with a touch of irony.

"Why not?" Pete asked back. "What's wrong with women like Kara?"

"People think I'm jealous of you," I said, sipping at my third pint. "But I don't think I'd want to have your life. No offence, but I just can't take children. I don't know how my life would turn if I'd got kids."

"Are you serious?" he said. "Having kids is the most fantastic thing on earth!"

"I don't know, man," I said. "The responsibility…"

He interrupted me: "Jerry, you have responsibility towards everyone you love. I mean, I'd die for my kids, I'd die for Kara and

I'd certainly die for you! But family is not just about blood. It's about loyalty."

He kept speaking, but I didn't listen further. Pete had said something that stuck in my head. Something about loyalty. 'Family is not just about blood'. Such a simple line, but it triggered something in my mind. I thought about Lucy and her quest to avenge her dead father. About Neville and the way he took me by his side, about the way he was using me to get back on top. And Martin Woodward saying he had been double crossed by someone he trusted.

"I'm sorry, Pete," I said, finishing my beer and getting up. "I have to go now."

He stared at me, surprised. "Where are you going?' he asked, a bit cross. "I thought you wanted to talk."

"Yes, but right now there are a couple of things I have to do," I said, and then added: "Thank you so much for what you have said."

"What?" he asked. "What do you mean?"

I smiled at him and said: "I think I've solved the case."

CHAPTER NINE

The Truth

"Wait a second!" said Neville. "Wait a second!"

He sat on a fallen trunk, breathless, and drank some water. I took the chance to do some stretching. The woods around us were dark and beautiful. We were surrounded by some of the most gorgeous landscapes the mountains of Scotland had to offer, but I was the only one enjoying it.

"When you said we would go trekking," he said, "I didn't think it would be so exhausting."

"You were the one who wanted to take a break from the TV cameras," I said.

"I was thinking of something different," he said. "We could have stayed in the lodge drinking beer and throwing darts. I'm not that young anymore. How long is this going to take?"

"See that stone?" I said, pointing to a big one halfway up the hill. "We got to get there!"

"Could I just die and you carry my corpse?" he asked.

"It's not that far," I said. "Come on, let's go."

He got up, bending over his trekking pole. Our holiday was going to be short: at the end of the week, Neville had to be back in London to meet the cast for the revival of *The Baker Street Sleuth*.

"I don't think you have seriously considered that role I offered you," he said as we walked.

"I'm no actor," I said. "And plus, I'm too young to play Watson."

"That's a shame," he said. "I really think you got what it takes."

"Save your breath for the walk."

Neville stopped again after a dozen steps. His face was red and dripping with sweat. He sat on the ground and drank the rest of the water in his canteen.

"That's it", he said. "No more trekking."

I took my backpack off and sat by his side.

"That's what happens when you smoke too much," I said.

"I quit smoking in real life," he said, and spat on the ground. "I just have that stupid pipe for the show."

"And for conventions," I said. "You smoke at conventions."

"Sometimes. But now in this revival we're shooting, they decided Sherlock Holmes shouldn't smoke. They say kids might start buying pipes if they relate to the character."

That revival was the talk of the town. There was a lot of money going around, and rumour was that Neville had signed contracts to appear in movies, TV commercials, videogames and even to have a series of toys with his face in it. After all that had happened, he was a bigger star than we could have dreamt.

"Now that we're here," I said, "there are a few things I wanted to talk to you about."

"Is it about TV?" he asked.

"No, it isn't about TV. It's about theatre."

"What about it?"

"*Who's Afraid of Virginia Woolf*," I said. "Do you remember it?"

His eyes filled with surprise.

"I've seen it, once or twice," he said.

"I know you did. At the Usual Company, maybe?"

I pulled a black and white photo from my pocket. Two actors, two actresses. The director was behind the camera.

"This guy here, playing Nick. His stage name is Manny Randel. His real name is Jordan Brown. I visited the Usual Company for the second time a few days ago, and this time the manager remembered you. You were part of the company for two years, long before you joined *The Baker Street Sleuth*."

He tried to get up, but his legs were shaking too much, and he sat down again.

"Don't try to run," I said calmly. "Even if you could get up, you're too old and tired to run."

"Jerry, please…"

"Manny Randel had a daughter," I said, talking over him. "To keep things simple, let's call her Lucy. Lucy was a young protégé of yours. You discovered her between rehearsals, when she came to visit her father, and decided to make a star out of her. Manny didn't like that idea very much, but you thought she had something special. You were her teacher.

"It took me a long time to piece this all together. It was only when I heard something about family that I was able to see the whole picture clearly. Lucy came to me to say that she was avenging the death of her father. So dramatic! A young girl who'd do anything for the memory of her father. It was all about family. But family is more than blood.

"This was all intuitive at first. I needed to back it up with facts. So I talked to actors, directors... Slowly a picture started to form in my head. I guess you and Randel were good friends, the kind that goes bowling every Saturday evening. He let you spend time with his daughter ever since she was a child. By the time you got him a role in *The Baker Street Sleuth* she was, what, sixteen? Seventeen?

"A girl like that, who dreams of one day becoming a great actress, would very easily be charmed by a veteran actor like you. And you took her under your wing, not to make her a star, but because you like to have people who adore you around. Too bad Lucy never made it big as an actress — she really had a great talent for it.

"But I think we both got Lucy wrong. She was determined to carry on with your orders, but at the same time she knew it was wrong. She knew what a viper you were, and tried to warn me not to get lost in your game the same way she did. She even threw a rock into my car to try and warn me. And that little touch with the panic button. It sure helped to build her character. I found this the last time I came to your house," I said, and reached for something in my pocket. I showed it to him: a small plastic device with a big red

233

button, just like the one Lucy had showed to me back in my flat. "It's your garage door remote control."

I put it back into my pocket. He had no way of denying it now. "Lucy was in love with you, wasn't she?" I said. "You were a god to her, and she would have done literally anything to be with you. Even…killing her own father? That was what I thought at first, but later I got another call from Mr Louvagh. He found out that Manny had died of cancer, five years ago, but the name that got to the papers wasn't Manny Randel, but Jordan Brown, his real name. If a fanboy like me hadn't known the second Watson had died, chances were very few people did.

"So Lucy's father was dead, but the world still thought the actor was alive. That meant you could fake his death, or even better, his murder! That was your plan, wasn't it? To create a fiction where you were a real detective in the real world, solving a real crime.

"It was just another convention for you, answering questions posed by hired actors. You knew where one of the actresses had to sit, so you instructed Lucy to take her place and ask about the murder of her father. The convention host was just as surprised as everyone else to hear those words. You probably had a dead man prepared for that moment, probably some John Doe at the morgue waiting to be identified as Manny Randel. Someone with his face destroyed by a gunshot or a fire, I don't know. His real name wouldn't matter that much; you'd be identifying him by his pseudonym. It would have been after his own daughter identified him. I don't know how the original plan went, and at this point it doesn't matter Lucy was to ask about her dead father. You were to accompany her in the investigations, find out who the killer was and, finally, get all the fame and glory. But you screwed that up when you lit that pipe, the same pipe you smoke at every convention. It set off the fire alarm, and interrupted your little act. That wasn't planned, was it? But you wanted to solve that real murder. What better way to do that than hiring a professional assassin under a fake name and later exposing him as the villain? That's when you got another brilliant idea: Lucy would call the police and say she saw a tall man pushing the alarm button. After that you only needed to find a tall man, hire him, plant some evidence and catch him later. He was the guy I fought at the hotel. He was no hitman, though. He was just an actor posing as such. I guess you have some sort of power over this kind of people. Just like Bill. We'll get to him in a moment.

"Anyway, after the convention. That's when I entered your life. I walked into your house, talking about the Watson killer, saying that we had to find him before he killed more people. It was like fate was making up for that fire alarm. Now you had a partner, and you could manipulate me to help you get into the press. But there was one thing I couldn't figure out. Why didn't Lucy use the name Randel when she talked about her father? Why Ferguson? Wouldn't it have made it more difficult for the world to know you were after the person who was killing Dr Watson? Then I realised: you didn't want to catch a serial killer, you wanted to catch a regular murderer!

"For as long as I live, I will regret having caused the death of all those men. I was the one who invented the Watson killer. It was all a product of my mind, created while I tried to find out who Lucy was. I came up with this crazy theory that Mark Duvall, the first Watson, had been killed by a mysterious psycho, when it was in fact just a regular burglary. And since Lucy had declared her father had been murdered, the idea didn't sound absurd at all.

"That day, I knocked at your door and told you my ideas. And you realised they were more promising than yours. Catching one murderer was good, but catching a serial killer? Wow! You already had a desperate man under your orders; all you needed to do was send him to kill a few specific people, and then later you'd catch him.

"At that moment, you made the transition from a crook to a murderer. I guess Woodward would have done anything for you at that point. He was desperate, after all, and you have that kind of power over people. No wonder he got so mad later when you double-crossed him. Was it hard to convince Lucy to make the transition, or was it as smooth to her as it was to Woodward? I don't know, and I don't want to know. You may think I'm a coward for wanting to keep her image pure in my mind. It's not real, but I think I deserve it.

"Bill and Martin Woodward, they weren't real either. Some more people from Sir Bartholomew Neville's court? Or just a couple of really desperate actors who'd do anything for a buck — even take part in this whole charade. They were acting, after all, and both did really well in their roles. The difference was that Bill got his way out of the whole thing before it was too late. Woodward was the real psychotic one. He wasn't going to let you get away with all this before giving him what you had promised.

"But I'm getting ahead of myself," I said, and tried to pick up my train of thought. "There was still a big problem in your way: how to find all those Watsons? You had no contact with them, and you needed someone who could find them before the police did, since they were no good to you if they were alive and talking. I was the best choice to locate those people, wasn't I? After all, I had no trouble finding you. You tell me to stay put, go upstairs, call Lucy and tell her to follow me to my house and seduce me, so you both can have more control over me. She was going to be my partner on that hunt, but somehow you were going to end up having all the credit. I had to lead you guys to the Watsons you couldn't find. And then you made it look like the tall man broke into your house and hit you as I was downstairs, just to keep me from suspecting you.

"And then you got too creative for your own good. You knew those men in black from your own racket, and you instructed them to do that silly secret agent act. You thought that that would confuse me enough so that I wouldn't think too much about it, and just do everything you told me to.

"Do you know what the major flaw in your plan was? People like me better than they like you. I was shocked when I realised it. Lucy started to care about me, and in a way so did Bill. They respected the way I was fighting against time to solve a case for which I wasn't getting a dime. You, on the other hand, were just a pompous prick, a stuck-up has-been who was manipulating them just as much as you were manipulating me.

"That's when Lucy decided she didn't want to deceive me any longer. She'd played the game really well thus far, pretending she wanted to kill you, when in fact she was helping you. But now she wanted to help me. I guess all those murders were starting to get to her, especially after you located Lewis Thompson and made her murder him, making it look like an accident. It really was a treat for you when I gave your address to Amanda Thompson, allowing you to burn the real memoir and forge a new one. I talked to her, by the way. She never had any intention of leaving town. She was also pretty mad to see us on national TV without giving her any credit, or, at least, some money.

"Anyway, you couldn't find Jake Scott by yourself. He could have been anywhere in the world. I guess the plan was for Lucy to follow me and kill him while I wasn't looking. I stayed with Scott at the motel, and Lucy came back later, with a black eye and a wounded leg. She was going to take us away, and I mean away from you. But I made her drive back to the motel, and the only way she could protect me was to kill Scott and disappear. And to think I was amazed that Woodward got there so fast after Scott got killed! He was there all the time; after all, he was the killer.

"At that point, I was aware of the information war. It was very intriguing. Bill told me a little more than you perhaps instructed him to, but that came in handy when you showed me the fake memoir of Lewis Thompson. Once again you were too creative, telling people Mortigan was the criminal mastermind behind it all. Even I bought it at first. Mrs Price told me little about her son, but one phrase stuck in my mind: 'he's gone crazy'. That's what she told me a few days before he died. But crazy how? Crazy for power? For blood? None of those. Unstable people go crazy after things go terribly wrong. Jay Mortigan wanted to be the boss of all crime in London in front of the camera, and for a little time he was. Now he's at a place called Alfred Adler Mental Hospital. He's been there for five years. He thinks he's Jesus, and the doctors say there is no cure for his illness. Mildred Hood said something about seeing him on TV, mugging for the camera. I don't know why he was on TV, but he wasn't mugging to give anyone any information. He actually was crazy.

"I know I've spent too much time in front of the TV. That's bad for your mental health. Makes you think the world has a regular three act structure, when in reality it doesn't. Makes you think crimes are committed by criminal masterminds, when in fact you got stupid people doing dangerous things. I look at you now and I don't see a man who's capable of doing all this. I don't see a man who would make a young girl kill a man and then commit suicide."

Neville kept his eyes on the ground as I said all that. As I made a brief pause, he sighed and then said in a sad voice: "It wasn't my idea. He...Woodward...the tall man. He wasn't just a frustrated actor. I met him at a boxing match, and Lucy thought we could manipulate him to do exactly what we wanted without question. You're right, he was crazy, and we didn't find it out until it was too late. We had planned to make it look like he was the murderer all the time. But the guy proved himself to be very smart. He wasn't the brains of the group, but he gave us a few ideas, and in the end he decided to take things in his own hands."

"He told me he wanted your head on a plate. How many lives are you going to destroy?"

"It's like you said, Jerry," he said, in a monotone. "I'm not a very bright person, and don't have much luck. All I wanted was to get back on top. We had a good plan, but it spun wildly out of control. He didn't have instructions to make Lucy kill herself; he just needed to shoot you. But that's what happens when the muscle of your operation grows some brains. He wanted Lucy dead to hurt me."

"If that's true, you acted splendidly when you saw her dead corpse in that kitchen," I said.

239

"And so did you," he said, with a somewhat evil smile. "You started to laugh so hard after you found that paint around her eye that I doubted you even liked her. It is a shame you won't get that role. Or maybe I should get you something a little more suitable to you, like Sebastian Moran."

"Stop with all that nonsense. I'm through with these games," I said, and then added, a bit randomly: "Sometimes the dead can be more sincere than the living, Bart."

"What do you mean?" he asked.

"Lucy knew she was going to die in that kitchen," I said. "And left me a message."

"What message?"

"Lucy killed herself by drinking the bleach because she wanted me to take a good look at her face. The day she came back to the motel, she had a black left eye. Her corpse had a black right eye. She was wearing stage makeup. But she was a continuity supervisor, wasn't she? I remembered something she said about never letting that kind of goof pass."

"That's right," he said, and then added with some pride in his voice: "She was the best I ever met. I got her a few gigs on the BBC."

"That's what I thought. It's unlikely that a continuity supervisor would make that sort of mistake. Unless, of course, she did it on purpose. It was a message, but it took some time to figure out what it meant. She was trying to tell me she wasn't a victim, but one of the villains. After that, every piece of the puzzle seemed to fit in its place. Except how you found Elroy."

"You won't believe it," Neville said. "He called me. He saw everything in the news and didn't call the police or the press. He called me. He wanted to be part of the show. Too bad for him that I already had a great Watson."

I looked at him and saw a fragile man, with shaking arms and sad eyes, eyes that didn't want to face me. So much had happened since I'd first praised that man like a god and later hated him like the devil. Now I just felt pity for him. He was a small person who'd tried to do something greater than himself, and now was the victim of his own naivety. So many people had died, so many lives wasted, and for what?

"You have a combination of words, don't you?" I said. "You have some key information that these important people want, and the best way to making lots of money with it is to be on TV all day, either on your show or giving interviews. That's why you've done all of this. That's what's behind this carnage."

"No," he said. "It's worse. I just wanted to get back on top."

I was holding my trekking pole so tightly it hurt my fingers, but when he said those words my hand lost its grip and it fell to the ground.

"There is no information war, Jerry," he said." It was just some crazy shit Bill made up from the top of his head to give the whole thing some sort of international intrigue feeling. He was always an ad-libber. That's why he never made it big. Do you really think they liked you by letting you know that bullshit? I guess you trust people too much. The truth is that I did get too creative. I was just an old fart who wanted to get back on top. And guess what? I've succeeded! The crazy, overcomplicated plan actually worked!"

241

I had no words.

"I guess people have done worse in their time," he said. "All I did was a jigsaw crockery routine. You make everything look bigger than it is, and the common mind will never figure it out. Except that you're not the common mind."

"So much death..." I said. 'So...so much..."

"Have you ever been loved by a country? A *whole* country? The day you have that kind of thing and lose it, you'll understand exactly why I did all of this. And now I guess my time has come," he said. "You didn't bring me here to the middle of nowhere just to tell me something you could have easily told me in a cosy and warm pub."

"You're right," I said. "I have no evidence to sustain this whole thing, which means that common justice won't touch you."

"I thought so."

"Aren't you going to fight me?" I asked.

"I can't. And I won't. You have worn me out in too many ways. Physically, mentally and spiritually. Anyway, I got what I wanted, and the only downside is that I won't live to enjoy it."

"Do you regret it?"

"Some of it, yes," he said. "I wish we had stuck to the original plan. It would have been cleaner and safer. I wish she hadn't died. She was the daughter I never had. And I wish I had told you everything from the beginning, instead of trying to use you like I did. We three could have had a lot of fun."

"I guess it's too late now, huh?"

"I guess so. But there is something I want you to remember for the rest of your days. If you hadn't given me so many great ideas, there wouldn't have been so much blood."

"Is that all?" I asked.

"Isn't it more than enough? You got a confession, a laugh and the final words of England's most famous actor. What else do you want, a glass of milk?"

"You should close your eyes."

And so he did.

EPILOGUE

My throat is dry and it's almost noon as I get to that point of my story. I had to call my office and tell them I was sick and couldn't go to work. My wife is concerned that I haven't eaten anything the whole day. I just ask her not to interrupt me, as I'm doing something very important. I don't expect her to understand it. After all, she met me after everything, years after the trial. There was no trace of the old Jerry Bellamy in me then. I was able to restart my life from scratch, and, with Pete's help, I went back to school and managed to build a good career.

I guess I also have to thank Pete for not being in jail right now. Many people wanted me behind bars for the murder of Bartholomew Neville. Pete got me the best lawyer in London and fully paid for his fees. In the end, it was proven that it was an accident that Neville fell off that cliff. My brother never stopped believing in my innocence, and I'd be lying if I said I didn't feel a bit guilty for that. Kara mustn't have liked it so much, and I guess that was the reason for their divorce.

I don't know what I'm going to do with this recording. Should I destroy it, like I said in the beginning? I don't know. Keeping it will be a big risk, even if I don't show it to anyone. These words are filled with anger and repressed thoughts, and I don't like to imagine how it'll be if my wife ever finds it. She knows something about my past, but there's so much I don't want her to know.

But I don't know if I can just press the erase button after everything I've just said. It'd feel like I was betraying myself. Not a day passes that I don't think about the whole thing, but this is the first time in so long that I actually examined it in chronological order.

So, the future of these recordings is unknown. I think I'll just leave them here for a while, until I decide what I'm going to do to them. I know no other way to finish this, except by saying that I met Bill again a couple of years ago. I was in Wales for business and had to stop for some petrol. I went to the petrol station toilets and there he was, dressed in a light blue uniform, unclogging a toilet. Our eyes met for a brief moment and I thought about saying hello, but then turned around and walked out of the door without washing my hands.

THE END

Also from MX Publishing

MX Publishing is the world's largest specialist Sherlock Holmes publisher, with over a hundred titles and fifty authors creating the latest in Sherlock Holmes fiction and non-fiction.

From traditional short stories and novels to travel guides and quiz books, MX Publishing cater for all Holmes fans.

The collection includes leading titles such as _Benedict Cumberbatch In Transition_ and _The Norwood Author_ which won the 2011 Howlett Award (Sherlock Holmes Book of the Year).

MX Publishing also has one of the largest communities of Holmes fans on _Facebook_ with regular contributions from dozens of authors.

www.mxpublishing.com

Also from MX Publishing

"Phil Growick's, 'The Secret Journal of Dr Watson', is an adventure which takes place in the latter part of Holmes and Watson's lives. They are entrusted by HM Government (although not officially) and the King no less to undertake a rescue mission to save the Romanovs, Russia's Royal family from a grisly end at the hand of the Bolsheviks. There is a wealth of detail in the story but not so much as would detract us from the enjoyment of the story. Espionage, counter-espionage, the ace of spies himself, double-agents, double-crossers...all these flit across the pages in a realistic and exciting way. All the characters are extremely well-drawn and Mr Growick, most importantly, does not falter with a very good ear for Holmesian dialogue indeed. Highly recommended. A five-star effort."

The Baker Street Society

www.mxpublishing.com

www.ingramcontent.com/pod-product-compliance
Lightning Source LLC
Chambersburg PA
CBHW071303250626
47159CB00004B/1291